THE LEDGER OF LIFE

*The Python Pit: The Complete Adventures
of Singapore Sammy, Volume 2*

BY GEORGE F. WORTS

A Queen of Atlantis

BY FRANK AUBREY

Four Corners, Volume 2

BY THEODORE ROSCOE

*The Stuff of Empire: The Complete Adventures
of Bellow Bill Williams, Volume 2*

BY RALPH R. PERRY

*Galloping Gold: The Complete Tales
of Sheriff Henry, Volume 4*

BY W.C. TUTTLE

*Jades and Afghans: The Complete Adventures
of Cordie, Soldier of Fortune, Volume 3*

BY W. WIRT

Minions of Mercury

BY WILLIAM GRAY BEYER

White Heather Weather

BY JOHN FREDERICK

*The Fire Flower and Other Adventures:
The Jackson Gregory Omnibus*

BY JACKSON GREGORY

THE LEDGER
OF LIFE

THE COMPLETE CABALISTIC
CASES OF SEMI DUAL, THE
OCCULT DETECTOR

J.U. GIESY & JUNIUS B. SMITH

ILLUSTRATED BY

SAMUEL CAHAN

COVER BY

ROBERT A. GRAEF

STEEGER BOOKS • 2020

TABLE OF CONTENTS

CHAPTER I

BLACKMAIL

BRYCE AND I were discussing routine matters of business in our suite on the seventh floor of the Urania Building, the day the thing began. Jim had been with the police, before he became my partner in our private detective venture, and there was still a decided air of the policeman about him. He was heavy-set, brown-haired, florid, as he faced me that morning, one of the deadly black cigars he affected clamped in his mouth, beneath his closely clipped mustache.

The inter-communication telephone interrupted our conversation, and I answered, to learn that a man by the name of Hendricks was in the outer office.

"Show him in," I directed, repeating the name to Jim.

"The broker?" he questioned and rolled his cigar across his mouth.

"I don't know—yet," I said.

The door of my private room opened and our visitor appeared. He was large—past middle age. But as he entered there was a suggestion about him of a body that had shrunken inside its carefully tailored clothing. It was like a human balloon, a trifle deflated by the loss of a part of its customary conceit.

"Hello, Jeff." Jim's greeting showed that he knew Hendricks.

"Good morning, Bryce," our caller returned, and seated himself. "I assume that anything I say will be considered confidential?"

Confusion reigned in the night club.

"Well, Glace and I aren't exactly a couple of he-gossips," Bryce returned.

"Then—here."

Hendricks extended an envelope which he drew from the inside pocket of his coat. Bryce took from it a single sheet of paper and shot his eyes along its typed lines and passed it to me.

"Uh-huh," he made non-committal comment. "Judgin' from your business, an' the side of the market you been playin', it looks like the big bear had stuck his foot in a trap."

Hendricks scowled, and I gave my attention to the note, which read:

DEAR MR. HENDRICKS:

I suppose now that Mrs. H. is home once more you're very happy. But I'm wondering if she would be equally so if the particular sort of tabloid which the *Prism* represents were to print the story of your conduct during the time she was out of town.

If you feel that the publication of such intimate details could not benefit any one save the *Prism*, perhaps you will be moved to take the steps which we now advise.

"She's—dead!" came a woman's gasping cry.

Place five hundred dollars in currency in an envelope, and have one of your regular messengers take it to the corner of Spring and Mason Streets to-morrow at exactly twelve noon. Tell him to hand it to the person who asks if he has a package to deliver. And please, Mr. Hendricks, be discreet. Any attempt to follow our messenger can only result in the very occurrence which our instructions are sincerely planned to prevent.

Trusting that you will display a better judgment now than in your association with the widow—

Confidentially—

ONE WHO KNOWS—ALL.

"POSSIBLY SOME one in the *Prism* office with a yen for a little easy money," I said as I folded the missive into its former creases.

"And how about the widow?" Bryce demanded. "How much dirt can the woman who wrote that spill?"

"Woman!" Hendricks repeated sharply. "You think a woman wrote it?"

"Well it sounds feminine—or feline—to me," Jim said. "Now, what about the widow?"

"Nothing, damn it!" Hendricks flushed. "I made an ass of myself, perhaps. We did a lot of business for her the past summer, and I—well—I played around with her a bit. But there was nothing to justify the implications of that filthy letter—which I admit would probably wreck my home if it were printed."

"Meanin'," said Jim, "that your wife would believe the worst?"

"She wouldn't pin any halos on me—and the hell of it is, I still love her!" Hendricks sighed. "So—I'm going to pay. And you're going to send somebody down to Spring and Mason, at noon, to spot whoever takes the money and see where it goes."

"Oh, yeah?" said Jim. "You think it will be that easy?"

"Easy or not, it's your job," the broker growled. "I'm paying, but only to shut their blackmailing mouths till you see whether you can put the finger on the writer of that note." His jaws set briefly before he went on. "Look, Bryce. It means a lot in my life."

I voiced a suggestion. "No chance that the widow could be mixed up in it herself?"

"What?" Hendricks stared. "Why—that's ridiculous! Some dirt artist has probably seen us in some night club."

"You took her to that sort of place?" said Bryce.

"Why not?" Hendricks challenged.

Bryce grinned. "I reckon the note is answer enough."

Hendricks bridled.

"Strikes you as funny, does it? Well, go on and laugh. All I want to know is whether you're going to have a man down there at noon to-day or not?"

"Why, sure." Jim drew his watch. "We'll have a good man there.—But don't expect immediate results. People who indulge in this sort of correspondence are pretty cagey. Probably about all we'll learn is the sort of bird who picks up your five yards.—An' here's a point: Their man probably knows your messengers by sight. They've sized up your office force in advance. But our man hasn't. So tell your boy to drop the envelope, when he hands it over, so that our man can spot the transfer. And—keep a record of the serial numbers of those bills. We'll keep the note.—And now you better be gettin' back to your sheep-shearin' pen, if you expect to deliver the wool at the time appointed."

Hendricks rose.

"Okay. Let me know anything you learn."

"Sure." Jim nodded assent. "Run along an' peddle your stocks."

HENDRICKS GOT himself out, and Bryce reached for the telephone and barked an order:

"Send Quinn in here."

I smiled. Out of such operatives as we controlled, I would have gambled on his choice. Danny Quinn had literally grown up with us. Bryce had recruited him as our office boy from the ranks of the city newsies, and had later dubbed him "The Young Sleuth" because of the natural aptitude he showed. He was slender, red-headed, agile and Irish. And there was little that escaped his flaring ears or his greenish-hazel eyes.

The latter fired with an unvoiced interest as he listened to Jim's explanation of his task.

"Okay!" He accepted it grinning. "I saw Hendricks come in, and I thought he looked like a guy what had sprained his confidence. I'll go down and see who drops that bundle of cabbage and who picks it up. Be seein' you later."

That was Danny always—casual as might be, but keen as a terrier for a scent; sophisticated; shrewd; and, young as he was, a post graduate in the many angles of modern city life.

When Dan had gone I looked at Jim. He shrugged.

"Yep. It looks like the big bear had put his foot in a trap," he remarked. "It's costin' him half a grand to-day, and it will cost him more unless we can pry him loose. This first five yards is just sugar."

"You still think a woman wrote this note?" I asked.

"Don't you?" he countered.

I nodded. There was a distinctly feminine flavor about the phrasing.

"Then that makes it unanimous," said Jim, and got out of his chair. "Let's go to lunch."

WE VISITED the little café where we generally ate, and we continued our discussion over our food. Then we came back. Dan had not returned, but as we passed through the outer office the girl at the telephone desk addressed me.

"Oh, Mr. Glace—there is a young woman in your room to see you."

"A young woman!" Jim repeated at my elbow. "Hendricks didn't say whether the widow was young or not."

"Think she may have got a note, too?" I smiled.

"She might have, at that," he said. "Blackmail is like blood to a sheep dog. Once you get a taste of it, you never know when to stop."

"Meanwhile, the young woman is waiting," I suggested, and opened the door of my private office.

A girl sat in a chair beyond my desk. She was slender, with bronze gold hair and blue eyes.

"Good afternoon," I said.

"Good afternoon," she said, in a nervous manner. "Are you Mr. Glace or—Mr. Bryce?"

"Glace," I told her, smiling.

"Then you're Mr. Bryce." She glanced at Jim and laughed. "I'm Allison Martin, and I'm jumpy as a fish. You see—yesterday I got a note—"

"A note?" Jim's tone was sharp, with the sharpness of surprise. "What sort of a note, Miss Martin?"

"Why—why—" she stammered, and opened a bag on her lap. "Here it is. I—brought it with me."

I took it and read it, with Bryce pressing against my shoulder to scan its typewritten lines.

DEAR ALLISON MARTIN:

Aren't you sometimes afraid that some one may tell your dear guardian that you are playing around with the gangster, Joe Palloni? And of what would happen if they did?

He's a racketeer you know, my dear—but not the only sort of racketeer. And all of us must live. So if you feel that your guardian might not approve of your recent association with Joe, just run a line in the personal columns of the *Record* saying "A.M. wishes to know what steps should be taken," and you will receive instructions as to how you should proceed to keep your indiscretions from coming to his ears.

It wasn't signed. But even so, I felt that in the abstract I knew its source. There was about it something of the same quality that had marked Hendrick's note—it was distinctly feminine in wording. That feeling I was once more unable to escape. Still—I got out the note which the broker had left and spread it on my desk beside the other. The typings, so far as I could see, was the same. The paper seemed the same in texture and weight.

BESIDE ME, Jim's breath rasped audibly in his throat.

"Looks like an epidemic," he grumbled.

"What?—An epidemic?" Miss Martin questioned.

"You're an orphan, Miss Martin?"

Jim swung to face her.

"Why, yes," she nodded. "But I'm of age. I can spend my own money if I have to. I—I'm afraid I've made a fool of myself. I've been majoring here at Sheraton College I met Joe Palloni, and I—well, it seemed sort of smart to play around with him. Only—Uncle Dick—that's what I call my guardian—is sort of old-fashioned. If he knew he'd throw a fit. I'd rather pay a little than to have him hear it. But I thought maybe I'd better see some one like you first. I—I think maybe I'm just a little bit frightened."

"Scared, huh?" Jim said.

"Yes, Mr. Bryce. You see, I—I showed that note to Joe Palloni last night, and I'm sure he knows who wrote it."

"Why?" Bryce snapped.

"Because"—the visitor caught her breath—"because of the way he acted after he'd read it. He—he grinned in a queer sort of way, and as he gave it back to me he said, 'Don't you worry, kid. If that biddy tries to muscle in on my prowls I'll put the heat on her myself.'—And how could he, unless he knows her?"

"Her, huh?"

Jim drew a cigar from his pocket and struck a match. There was a covert satisfaction in his face—a sort of quiet gloating that I myself could comprehend, in view of what the slender blond girl had just said. With deliberate care, Jim fired his dark roll of tobacco.

"Yes, sir," Miss Martin replied. "At least that's exactly what Joe said."

"Uh-huh," Jim grunted. "I don't doubt it.—Listen, Miss Martin.—You ain't the only one who's been getting notes. Yours is the second one we've had the pleasure of reading to-day. And if Palloni said what you say, I wouldn't be in a hurry to put anything in the paper. Men like Joe don't pull that sort of thing unless they know what they're talking about. So just leave us your address, and the note, in case we need to use it. Then do what he said—don't worry."

"But I can't help it!" Miss Martin protested. "I—you see, I'm afraid I may not have been wise in showing it to him. I know blackmailing isn't a very nice business; but I wouldn't want anything terrible to happen to whoever wrote that because of me. And the way Joe looked, for just a minute, when he read it— You don't suppose he meant anything like that, do you, Mr. Bryce?"

"No," Jim told her, "I don't. He probably meant that he'd warn her to let you alone, unless she wanted something a lot like trouble. I'd advise you to run along and leave her to Palloni—and leave Palloni to us."

"Oh—I see."

Miss Martin rose. And all at once she smiled.

"You mean if Joe knows her," she added, "you can make

him tell you who she is. And if she wrote the other note you mentioned—"

"Here, here!" Jim interrupted, grinning. "You aren't a detective, young woman. But anyway that's a thought."

Miss Martin giggled, and as she made her exit gave me her address.

BRYCE CHUCKLED when she had disappeared.

"Funny how, sooner or later, they always trip themselves," he said. "She picks on this kid, and she shows the note to Palloni. She ain't dumb, if she is good looking. Well Gordon, old son, it looks like we get a break. If both of them notes wasn't typed on the same machine, my eyesight's failing. And if Palloni knows the dame what wrote 'em—"

He broke off as Dan opened the door and came in with his hat on the side of his head and a question in his eyes.

"Who was the wren who just flew out of here?" he asked, as he took a chair.

Rather to my surprise, Bryce told him.

Danny nodded when he paused. "At that rate, it looks like we might be able to play both ends of the thing against the middle," he declared. "I spotted the rat what picked up Hendrick's five yards. And rat is right. He looked like a chorus man or a gig, or somethin' of that sort. You know—dark and slender, and thin-faced, and clever on his feet. He glaums the kale off Hendrick's man and beats it for the *Prism* office like a shot."

"The *Prism?*" I echoed sharply.

"Yeah." Quinn grinned. "Looks like a natural, don't it, consid-erin' how a lot of these tabloid dirt hounds make a bit of side money, all the time, by suppressin' stuff that ain't too important to be suppressed—except to the party they've hung it on. Of course, I ain't sayin' Hendricks is up against that racket. I don't know whether the rat left the money in that scandal mill or not. I tailed him as far as I could, and then I waited till he showed again, and followed him to the Silver Moon—if you know the hush hut I mean—"

I nodded. I knew it, all right. The Silver Moon was a night club of the more opulent sort—a place of black and silver trimmings, of black and silver shadows, of a glittering bar after the European fashion, of a main room with a dance floor and tables and wall seats, and overhead a painted sky in which by means of a clever lighting effect a moon was from moment to moment obscured or revealed by a semblance of floating clouds.

There were no windows in the black and silver paneled walls of the place, nor any need of them. Black and silver fabrics draped the walls. And the moon was a trick moon inasmuch as it followed the actual phases of the luminary which it mimicked, from hour to hour. Sometimes it was new, and sometimes it was full, and sometimes there was no moon at all.

"And that's all?" I said.

"Yep, that's all," Danny agreed. "Except that I'd thought of goin' down there to-night and see if the rat is part of the floor show."

"Which wouldn't surprise me, either," said Jim. "His stopping in at the *Prism* might be just a stall. You know, the dame who wrote that letter told Hendricks not to follow the mug who took the money. Havin' him drop in at the *Prism* would be a good way of scarin' off pursuit—if any."

"Dame, huh?" Danny eyed him.

"Yeah," Bryce stood his ground. "Leastwise, it strikes me as the sort of stuff a dame might write."

"Well then," Danny rose, "unless you object, I'm goin' to see if I can spot this bird to-night."

"You and us, both," Jim amended. "We'll got with you, and then if you spot him you can point him out."

CHAPTER II

UNDER SUSPICION

I SHALL NEVER forget that night. Danny and Bryce and I reached the Silver Moon at an hour when its hectic night life was at its height. We gave our order, and sat there at a little table in the black and silver room, our backs to the wall. Music throbbed and men and women were dancing.

There was no hint of the gruesome thing impending. The "moon" in the painted sky was at its "full," and a number of the floor show was in progress. A score of slender young women clad in little more than moonbeams were posturing to music as soft as the pulse of a moonlit surf.

I gave particular attention to their leader, because in her revealing beauty she was undeniably a thing of grace.

Then Jim brought me back to the purpose of our visit.

"There's Palloni!" he exclaimed.

I followed his glance, to a table where two men and two women sat. The latter were of a type it was easy to recognize, and I gave my attention to their masculine companions. Palloni I knew by sight, as overlord of the underworld the past few years. He was dark, clean shaven, heavy set, and perfectly groomed. A cigar was thrust between his vulpine lips.—Vulpine, I thought, was a suitable word; for he was like a sleek and well fed wolf as he sat there, an undisputed leader of his pack.

The other man I did not know. He was younger, thin faced, thin lipped, with dark eyes and heavy, inky brows. Both men were watching the professional dancers with the expression

11

that comes over most men when they gaze on a bulk of feminine flesh.

"Who's the other one?" I asked.

"Search me!" Jim shook his head.

Dan beckoned a waiter over. "Who's the guy with Palloni?"
he inquired.

"Tommy Tovallo," the man said, with no sign of hesitation.

"Nice baby!" Dan said when the waiter had retired. "They
say he's one of Joe's choppers. Maybe that's where they get the
'tommy' part of it. Tommy-gun, you know. Hey—hold everything—" His voice grew tense. "There's the rat—at Palloni's
table!"

The dancers were withdrawing to a tap of drums, and a man
had paused at the gangster's table. He was dark and slender,
as Dan had said. In the lapel of his dinner jacket was a garde-
nia. I saw him speak to Palloni and Tovallo; then, as the music
changed and our waiter came with our order, I saw one of the
women at Palloni's table rise and take her place beside the man I
was watching. He led her onto the floor, upon which the patrons
were beginning to revolve to the urge of a half barbaric rhythm.

"Who's the gig with the flower?" Danny drawled.

"Giovanni Cerra, sir," our waiter answered. "But we generally
call him Jumping Jack, or Johnny."

"Regular here?" Dan prompted.

"Yes, sir."

THE LIGHTS went down. The moon faded out. A shadowy
dusk filled the black and silver room. Beyond us the crowd on
the floor were no more than shifting shadows that swirled in a
rhythmic sequence to the staccato beat of drums.

"Clever trap this," said Bryce. "You know, Palloni owns it.
Every time that trick moon goes 'dark' they have one of these
jungle dances."

His description struck me as apt. I had already marked the
primitive quality of the music, in which the drums were heavily

emphasized. With their constant thud and tap they were not unlike tom-toms in a jungle.

"The rat's a gig, all right." Satisfaction marked Jim's voice. "And he knows Palloni well enough to be dancin' with one of his women."

"Couldn't be workin' a blackmailing racket with her, could he?" Dan voiced a suggestion.

"With one of Joe's twists? You're dizzy!" Jim growled.

"Well, the Martin kid seemed to think Joe knew who wrote them notes," Quinn said.

"Hey—wait a minute!" Jim scowled.

And it was then that tragedy stalked.

The lights came on. There was now a new moon in the painted sky. The dancers streamed back to their tables and—a woman screamed!

At first it was just an inarticulate cry of horrified realization. And then words followed:

"Margaret! Mar—garet!— Dick! Bob!— She's—dead! Oh—God!"

For an instant heavy silence—and then confusion reigned. Men and women turned in that black and silver scene of pleasure to stare at the girl who stood with a white, white face at a corner table. They began to murmur, to mutter, to crowd in upon her.

Jim's police experience came to the fore.

"Quick, Dan!" he hissed. "Get back to the door an' tell 'em not to let anybody out!—Come on, Gordon."

He drove straight for the table where, as I followed, I saw that the girl who had screamed had sunk down at the side of another woman whose body sagged on the seat in the angle of the walls.

VAGUELY, AS we made our way toward her, I realized that this woman was truly dead. I saw a man in evening dress reach the table and speak to the girl beside her. And I saw the second girl lift her eyes.

"She's—dead, Dick," I heard her stammer as we hurried up. "There's—blood on her gown!"

"Just a minute," Bryce took charge. "What's happened? I'm a detective."

The man turned his eyes. Later, we knew him as Richard Torrance.

"I don't know," he said "Gladys, try to get control of yourself."

"I—can't." The girl's chin quivered. She half screamed again. "Bob!—Bob O'Neil! Oh—Bob!"

A second man, large, broad shouldered, fair, burst through the growing press about us.

"Oh—Bob—!" she faltered. "She's—dead!"

I saw that her hair was a deep auburn and that her horror-widened eyes were gray.

"Margaret!" The man whom the girl had addressed as Bob laid hold of the table and flung it to one side. He went to his knees before the dead woman, who sat with her shoulders wedged into the angle of the walls. He caught up her hand.

"Margaret!—Margaret! It's Bob. Margaret—speak to me!" he begged.

In the crowd about us a woman sobbed; and for the first time I heard Joe Palloni's voice. He shouldered in beside us, his cigar still in his mouth.

"Hello, Bryce," he spoke around it. "What's the trouble?"

Jim answered in a lowered voice. "Reckon that girl in the corner's dead, Joe. There's blood on her dress and—it's over her heart. Looks like a police job. Shall I handle it for you?"

"Yeah." Palloni nodded, and stepped onto the seat along the wall, to face the mass of startled men and women.

"Listen, folks. Somethin's come off here, but we ain't sure what—just yet. Play the game, willya, an' go back to your tables an' keep still till we get the low down on it. Come on now, please!"

For a moment nothing happened except that Bryce hurried

away in search of a telephone; and then the crowd began to drift back to their tables. All save one man, who stood fast. He was an individual with an almost colorless, though well featured and intelligent, face. He had a certain confident, self-assured poise. I recognized him as a lawyer by the name of Richfield.

"Hello, Joe," he tossed a greeting to Palloni, and spoke to the man who still knelt beside the dead woman. "Come, O'Neil. Pull yourself together."

"But—she's dead! They—killed her!"

O'Neil turned haggard eyes.

"Who killed her?" Palloni demanded.

"I—don't know."

O'Neil rose slowly; appeared to stumble. For an instant I thought he was going to fall. Then he caught himself, stooped and groped on the floor, to straighten again with a gun in his hand.

"Whoever this belongs to," he added, with a sudden grit in his voice.

IT WAS a thirty-eight caliber gun, equipped, as I saw, with a silencer. And in a flash I saw more. I saw how the whole thing might have happened. The room had been dark. There had been that thud and tap of drum, which, to unsuspecting ears, might well have masked the sound of the muffled shot.

I caught a napkin from a table and took the deadly little weapon from O'Neil's grasp.

"Careful or you'll destroy any marks it may have on it," I said, and dropped it into my pocket.

"Hey—just a minute! Who are you?" Palloni rasped.

"Glace. Bryce and I are partners," I told him.

"Oh—another dick."

He nodded.

"Know the girl?" I asked.

"Sure," he said. "She's Margaret Kenton. Runs the Kenton

Reporting Bureau, in the Meehan Building. She used to work for Richfield. Helluva break, ain't it?"

"Not so good," I said, and glanced at Richfield.

He was speaking in lowered tones to the auburn-haired girl and O'Neil and Torrence. He appeared to know the lot of them. I saw him bend over and eye the little spot of blood on the dead girl's gown.

Danny came back with Jim.

"I got Johnson," the latter said, "an' he's bringin' a doctor."

I nodded. Detective Inspector Johnson had been Jim's friend, before Bryce had left the police to come in with me; and we had worked together on more than one case since. He was a sincere and dependable man.

I described the finding of the gun. Richfield heard me, and joined us.

"See here," he said. "The cloth around the hole in her gown is—scorched."

"Meanin' she might have done it herself?" Jim grunted.

Richfield shrugged. "The—er—fact seems suggestive."

"Well, then—while she was doin' it where was the lad who's sittin' beside her now?" said Dan.

"He says he'd gone to the check room. And if you'll remember, he came up after Miss Ingham screamed," the lawyer returned.

"That's right," I agreed.

Outside, the shriek of a police siren rose in approaching crescendo, gasped, and died. Johnson came in, with a detective sergeant and a bruskly professional third party.

"What you dug up?" he inquired as the latter advanced to begin a medical examination.

We told him, and I gave him the napkin-wrapped weapon.

"Here, Reilley, see if this is registered, will ya?" he said, and handed it to the sergeant.

Reilley went out, and Johnson glanced at the police surgeon. The physician shook his head.

"Straight through the heart—and close. The cloth is scorched," he announced.

JOHNSON SEATED himself on a corner of a table. "Just the four of you in your party?" he asked.

"Yes," O'Neil assented.

"And—you found the gun?"

"Yes. It was on the floor."

"And how did you know where it was?"

For a moment the glances of the two men held, before O'Neil answered.

"I—stepped on it when I tried to get up."

"An' where was you when it happened?" Johnson asked.

"At the check room," O'Neil told him. "Gladys and Dick were dancing, and Margaret wanted her compact. Said she'd dropped her bag into my overcoat pocket. She often did that. I went to get it—"

"This it?" The surgeon held up a woman's bag, a rather elaborate affair.

"Why—yes."

O'Neil hesitated briefly in his answer. He seemed surprised.

"And I suppose you tucked it down between her and the wall after you got it for her?" the surgeon snapped.

"But—he couldn't have done that!" the girl we were to know as Gladys Ingham broke in to protest. "Besides—"

She caught her breath with an audible gasp.

"Besides what?" Johnson demanded. "Come on, young woman."

"Why—why—I was only going to say that—Margaret had her bag with her all along," the girl half panted.

"Well—?" Johnson swung his glance to O'Neil again. It almost seemed to accuse.

Yet O'Neil met it without flinching.

"Miss Ingham is probably right. I—failed to find the bag

in my overcoat pocket, and then this happened. It must have happened while I was at the check room."

Johnson's words came charged with meaning. "Any reason why it couldn't have happened *before* you went out there?"

O'Neil's lips twisted to show clenched teeth. "Nobody but a cop would intimate that I might have—murdered the girl I— expected to—marry," he said in a voice that broke on the last word.

"Bob!" The auburn-haired girl put out a hand to touch him.

Reilley came up and spoke to Johnson in a voice so low I could not catch the words. But I marked their effect on the inspector.

"On the level?" I heard him rasp.

As Reilley nodded, he slipped off the table to stand upon his feet. His eyes swung from O'Neil to the body of Margaret Kenton. His expression struck me as blank.

"What's the matter, inspector?" Richfield asked.

"Why—" Johnson turned to face him, and his lids were narrowed, "it's like this, Mr. Richfield. The gun's registered, all right, and, accordin' to our records, it's—hers."

CHAPTER III

JUMPING JACK

"YOU MEAN MISS Kenton's," Richfield said. "I know she bought one some years ago, because her permit was granted on my recommendation. But I'd forgotten, for the minute. So if the gun was hers, and it was found lying at her feet, and if her gown was scorched, doesn't it occur to you, inspector, that it may have been—er—self-destruction?"

Johnson scowled. His voice was harsh. "No, it don't. Pickin' this place, an' puttin' a silencer on her cannon, is too funny a form of suicide. Reilley, where's that gat?"

"Here, sir." The sergeant produced it.

Johnson took it, still in the napkin which I had wrapped about it. With a sudden gesture he thrust it beneath Bob O'Neil's eyes.

"Is this her gun?" he rasped.

"I don't know," O'Neil made sullen answer. "I know she had one like it."

"And a silencer to fit it?"

"I don't know, inspector. I never saw one."

"But you saw the gun?"

"Oh, yes." Bob O'Neil sighed.

"Where?"

"In her rooms, inspector."

"Would that mean you knew where she kept it?" Johnson snarled.

"Certainly. She had it in the upper drawer of an old highboy in her bedroom."

"An'—you wasn't there before you come here to-night?"

"But I was," O'Neil contradicted. "The four of us met there. See here, if you think I had anything to do with what's happened, why don't you take me where we can go into this in private?"

"Bob!" Gladys Ingham admonished. "You mustn't talk like that."

"No?" He gave her a glance. "I'm talking to a policeman, Gladys, and in such cases you can't appeal to reason or intelligence."

The thing was poorly judged, of course. But I could understand why the man was on edge. Color crept into Johnson's cheeks, but he agreed with O'Neil's suggestion.

"An' that might not be a bad idea, either. We'll take you and these friends of yours along for a little talk. All right, Joe," he addressed Palloni. "Let the rest of the folks here go. We'll have the body moved at once. But your show's over for to-night."

O'Neil caught a rasping breath. "One moment, inspector," he begged. "Don't take her to—the morgue. Take her to a mortuary. I—I'll stand good for anything that's needed."

Johnson eyed him. "Okay," he conceded at length. "See to it, Reilley. And the rest of you, come along."

As Gladys Ingham rose, Richfield spoke to O'Neil.

"I wouldn't make any more cracks, to-night, my boy. But I was Margaret's friend, and I'll be glad to act as your attorney unless you have a different choice."

"Thank you, sir," O'Neil said, dully.

We filed from the black and silver room, O'Neil with a lingering glance at the girl he loved.

OUTSIDE JOHNSON spoke to Bryce as the two men and the girl took places in a police car. "Thanks, Jim, for holdin' the lid on till I got here. Know anything, or did we get it all?"

"All to date, anyway," Jim replied. "Okay." Johnson stepped into the car. " 'Night."

"So long," said Bryce as the car shot away with a reawakened siren. "Come along," he prompted.

"Where?" I asked.

"Inside." He gave me a glance. "We come down to check on that gig, not to attend a murder."

Beside me, Danny Quinn snickered as we fought our way in against the stream of patrons hurrying out.

"Reilley was waiting beside the body.

"I want to see Palloni," Jim explained, and repeated the words to a waiter, who hurried off.

We seated ourselves at a table. Three or four minutes passed. At their end, Palloni came toward us, with a fresh cigar in his mouth.

"Rotten business, huh?" he remarked.

"Oh, I don't know," said Bryce. "Folks will want to see where it happened. You'll probably need extra help to-morrow night."

A slow grin of understanding twitched the gangster's mouth.

"Well, maybe," he assented. "You wanted to see me?"

"Yeah." Jim nodded. "You got a gig you call Jumpin' Jack around here?"

"Johnny." Palloni's brows knitted in a momentary frown. "An' so what?"

"Where is he?" Bryce asked.

"Search me." Palloni shifted his glance about the room. "Gone home, maybe. He was dancin' with one of the dames in my party, just before the Kenton twist was bumped off."

"I seen him," said Bryce.

"Then what's the idea in askin'?" Palloni gave him a coldly level glance.

"Mainly that I didn't see him *after* the shootin'," Jim replied.

Palloni's frown deepened. "Now—wait a minute!" he protested. "Johnny's been round here a coupla years—"

"An' you know him pretty well, huh?" Bryce suggested. "Maybe you know if there was anything between him and the Kenton kid."

"HELL!" PALLONI'S response was a thing of profane disgust.

"You're washed up, Bryce. He's got a doll of his own. Say—did Johnson tell you to ask me that?"

"Nope. I thought it up all by myself," Jim sneered. "Now listen, Joe. If he's around here, dig him up."

"Okay." Palloni shrugged. "This ain't the first time you dicks have guv me a laugh."

He signaled the waiter who had taken Jim's message to him.

"See if you can find Johnny," he directed, and turned back to Jim. "On the level, Bryce, Johnny was dancin' when it happened—"

"Yeah," Bryce agreed. "An' the room was dark, an' the drums was makin' plenty of noise, an' the gun had a silencer on it.— Somebody burned her."

"She could have done it herself," Palloni snarled.

"Yeah." Jim nodded. "But where was the sense in her comin' here to do it? Look, Joe—what do you know about her?"

"Nothing more than I told your partner here." Palloni shifted his eyes to me. "She's been comin' here a lot, an' mostly the Ingham frail an' that fella Torrance came with her."

"An' O'Neil," Jim amended.

"Oh—him. Sure." Palloni laid his index and middle finger together. "They was like that," he added.

"Did Cerra know her?" Joe inquired.

"Sure," Palloni told him. "I've seen him dancin' with her sometimes, when she come in alone. You know we run a cocktail dance in the afternoon."

The waiter returned. "I can't find him, boss," he reported.

Bryce nodded. "Know where he lives, Joe?" he questioned.

"Sure."

Palloni mentioned an address not far from the Silver Moon.

"Goin' to see him?" he asked, in a slightly too casual tone.

"I don't know. I might."

Jim rose.

"It would depend on whether he knew I was comin' before I got there or not," he finished.

Palloni nodded. "Sometimes," he said, "you're almost smart, for a cop."

"An' sometimes for a gorilla who's aced himself up the way you have, you're almost dumb," Jim returned. " 'Night, Joe."

"And now what?" I demanded, as we went to my parked car.

"Drive to that address Joe just gave us," Bryce requested. "We'll see if Johnny is home. It's sort of funny, his pickin' up Hendrick's money—an' Palloni sayin' he'd put the heat on whoever was musclin' in on his prowl. Then Cerra's bein' a gig in Joe's trap—an' the Kenton twist bein' cooled.— What did Joe tell you about her?"

I GAVE him the information briefly, and he grunted.

"Run a stenographic service, did she, an' worked for Richfield before that, an' used to dance with Cerra? Did either of you see a sign of him after the shootin'?"

"Personally, I never thought of him after the murder was discovered," I returned.

"Neither did I," said Dan. "The last thing I saw of the rat was when he started to dance with that doll at Palloni's table. Could Joe have engineered the whole thing? He seemed sorta nervous to me, just now. D'ye reckon Joe meant this Kenton girl when he was talkin' to the Martin kid?"

"I ain't puttin' out nothin'—yet," said Jim. "I ain't really begun to think."

"But—" Dan's tone was eager—"if she run a stenographic business, she could have written—"

"She could have written anything," Bryce interrupted. "Step

on it, Gordon, will ya? If the Jumpin' Jack is home, we'll see what he's got to say about Margaret Kenton—or if he'll say anything."

"You're not seriously considering Dan's suggestion, are you?" I said, and let in the clutch.

"Well, somebody killed her for a reason," Bryce rejoined. "An' blackmail is sometimes a risky game. Those notes looked to me like the work of a woman—and—"

"To-night," I threw in, "she was killed with her own gun."

"With a silencer on it," Bryce added. "It's the silencer makes me so dead sure it's murder, old son."

"The Ingham frail mighta done it," said Dan. "Give a look, now. Say she was jealous. She's stuck on O'Neil, unless I'm blind. Look how she acted to-night. An' accordin' to O'Neil, the four of them met at the Kenton doll's flop. Suppose Ingham knew where she kept that gun. She coulda glaumed it easy by goin' into the bedroom to powder her nose before they went to the Moon. She coulda took it with her an' plugged the Kenton dame—"

"While she was dancin' with Torrance?" said Jim.

"No, afterwards. It woulda been only a matter of seconds, and—he wasn't with her," Dan declared. "I know, because I seen him dashin' away from a table. And then, when I come back with you after you'd called Johnson, there he was."

"That's right," I agreed. "He was there when you and I reached the table, Jim. But he wasn't there when she screamed. I saw him run up from somewhere."

"An' here we go, draggin' in the old triangle again," Jim said in an injured tone. "There's been a lot of sad tunes played on the thing since the days of Adam. But that girl didn't act to me like a dame who had just cooled her rival."

"Maybe that was because she *was* actin'," said Dan as I brought the car to a stand.

"Yeah," Jim said as we got out. "An' I reckon the trouble with you is you've been goin' to too many picture shows. You sound like one of them plots."

WE FOUND the number we wanted, over the entrance to a stairway, and mounted to a dingy "office" where a sleepy-eyed youth was lolling in a chair.

"He ain't in yet, or if he is, I didn't see him come in," he replied to Jim's inquiry for Cerra, and mentioned the number of the room. "You can go up if you want to."

We mounted another flight of stairs, passed down a corridor, and paused before one of the flimsy doors. Bryce rapped. Footsteps sounded from the room. The door was drawn partly open by a blond woman clad in a cheap kimona.

"Johnny in?" Bryce answered the unspoken question of her china blue eyes.

"Nope." Her voice was flat in denial. "He ain't here, mister."

"Expectin' him, ain't you?" Bryce inquired.

"What's it to you?" the woman rejoined. "Say—what's the notion?"

"Well," Bryce informed her, "the notion is, we're a number of dicks."

"An' you think Johnny knows somethin' about that shootin' at the Moon?"

All at once the woman's tone was sharp.

"What do *you* know about it?" Jim returned. "Or did Palloni tip Johnny off that wc was comin'?"

"Say—listen," the girl protested. "I don't know a thing. Did Joe know you was lookin' for Johnny?"

"Behave!" said Bryce. "If you wanta talk, why don't you ask us in?"

"Why, sure." The woman stepped back. "But it won't do you any good."

"If it don't, we can find our way out," Jim said as he led the way inside.

We glanced around. There was little to see—just a bedroom, a kitchenette, a living room. Jim made the circuit of them while the woman watched. She was as slender as a boy, I noticed, and with a subtle grace of body and limb.

"Okay, sister," Bryce said at length. "I don't seem to find him, either."

"Know who that was?" I asked as we regained the street.

"Sure. She's the Jumpin' Jack's moll," Jim returned.

"She's more than that," I told him. "She's Joe's *première danseuse*—the girl who was leading the floor show when we went into the Moon to-night."

"Sure," Danny Quinn agreed, with a tense note in his young voice. "I knew her the minute I lamped her. And what does that add up to?"

"Write your own ticket," said Bryce, in a somewhat grumpy tone.

CHAPTER IV

COMPLICATIONS

QUITE UNEXPECTEDLY, GLADYS Ingham came to our
office the next morning.

The papers carried a full account of the tragedy of the night
before. According to them. O'Neil was now in jail as a suspect.
There was a brief resume of the dead woman's life. But beyond
what we had gained, it gave me no information, except for a
single item which I later mentioned to Bryce.

I had barely finished my mail when he strolled into my private
room and flopped himself into a chair. "Seen the papers?" he
inquired.

"Naturally," I returned. "I see the Kenton woman was
formerly a court reporter."

"Yeah." Jim bit the end from a cigar. "I reckon she's been a lot
of things.—Johnson's frothing at the mouth. Last night, after
he'd finished with O'Neil an' the Ingham girl and Torrence, he
takes it into his head to look at the dead girl's flop. He goes over
to the Willden Apartments with Reilley, about two o'clock. An'
the first thing they find is the end of a suit of step-ins, stickin'
out of a drawer in that chest of drawers in her bedroom where
O'Neil says she kept her gun. Only it was stickin' outa the *bottom*
drawer, when, accordin' to O'Neil again, she kept the gat in the
top.

"Well, they examine this drawer an' they find it's got a double
bottom. There's ain't nothin' in it, and so Johnson is wonderin' if
there ever was, or if somebody outfoxed him last night and went

through the dump before he got there. He says if they did, they knew where to look for what they went for, because there wasn't anything else disturbed."

"And nothing to show, I suppose, that the girl might not have shut the drawer on a bit of her lingerie herself?" I smiled.

"Nope." Bryce grinned. "There's something clever or crazy about this business, son. The gig wasn't in his flop when we stopped there."

"Still chewing on Dan's idea of a hook-up between last night and those notes?" I questioned.

"Dan's no fool," Jim said. "I trained him. An' blackmail's been known to lead to dirty work. It looks like the Kenton girl had been put on a spot.—Gimme the phone. I got to call Hendricks and tell him we got a line on the man who picked up his jack."

It was while he was speaking with our client of the day before that the house phone buzzed and Miss Ingham was announced.

I waited until Bryce had finished his conversation and had shown her in.

THAT SHE had regained her self-control I saw the moment she entered. And I met a surprise in the way she accepted a seat and instantly came to the point.

"Good morning, gentlemen. I want to see you on behalf of Bob O'Neil. I suppose you know they are holding him for Marge Kenton's murder—and I'm afraid that it's partly my fault. But I was so terribly shocked when I came back from dancing with Dick—I mean Mr. Torrance—and found her dead.—And then when that policeman, Johnson, seemed so determined to fasten it on him, I—well, I rather lost my head. Bob never did it, of course—and I asked Inspector Johnson about you last night. I want you to find out who really did kill Marge."

"And—how about O'Neil?" I asked. "Does he feel the same way about it, or are you coming to us on your own account?"

"He knows I'm coming." She breathed deeply and set her lips. "But really he doesn't care about himself. He's terribly broken up. They let me talk to him last night, and I don't care how that policeman makes it look—or tries to—Bob's innocent. You see I worked for Marge Kenton, and I knew her. I know Bob, too, and I'd do anything for him. Like all real men, he's somewhat simple. I suspect that's why he never picked Marge for what she was. I know that sounds rotten, after what's happened. But—"

"Well, what was she?" Bryce cut her short.

For a moment she did not answer, and then she shrugged.

"Almost everything except what he thought—she was cold, calculating, selfish. And—she owned him, body and soul." She broke off with a nervous laugh. "Of course I'm prejudiced!" she added.

"Well, if we go into this for O'Neil, I don't know that your prejudice will prove an objection," Jim said dryly. "But you don't want to be too hard on Johnson. He's one white cop. Did he know you were coming to us?"

"No." Miss Ingham shook her head. "I merely asked him who you were. And then I suggested coming to Bob, and we decided to ask you to see what you could do."

"Uh-huh." Jim nodded. "In sayin' you worked for Miss Kenton, do you mean in her stenographic business?"

"Yes, Mr. Bryce—in the office."

"And would that mean that you knew quite a bit about her personal affairs?"

"It—might." Miss Ingham's tone was guarded.

Bryce grinned. "Then would you mind tellin' us whether you know a gigolo called the Jumping Jack or not?"

"Jumping Jack?" Gladys Ingham repeated quickly. "Why, of course. He—works in the Silver Moon. He was there last night."

"And did Miss Kenton know him?"

"Certainly."

Bryce nodded. His manner altered.

"See here, Miss Ingham," he demanded. "Was Madge Kenton workin' a blackmailin' racket?"

"BLACKMAIL?" OUR visitor parroted, and paused. I saw

a startled look of conviction in her eyes. And suddenly a faint smile suggestive of nothing so much as a glutting vengeance sat briefly on her lips.

"Why, I—I never thought of that. But now that you suggest it, it wouldn't surprise me. Do you mean that Jumping Jack was mixed up in it, too, Mr. Bryce?"

But Bryce refused to answer. "Why wouldn't it surprise you?" he asked.

"Why—" the girl hesitated briefly. "Why—because of things I've seen and heard. The Jumping Jack was always coming to the office. Sometimes he'd be in her private office for an hour or more before he left.—And there was our business. It's fallen off badly of late. But Marge always seemed to have plenty of money, and a few weeks ago she told me she was expecting to come into what she called a small fortune. She said that when she got it she was going to marry Bob and go to Europe."

"Isn't O'Neil in a position to support a wife?" I questioned.

"That would depend on the woman he married, I guess," Miss Ingham replied. "He's a bond salesman, you know; and you know that isn't much good of late. Anyway, it wasn't support Marge wanted. She wanted to be rich enough to do anything she pleased."

"So do I," said Jim. "But let it pass.—Ever see any letters or papers that would look suspicious?"

"No," Miss Ingham replied. "I wasn't in her confidence to that extent. I don't think anybody was. Marge was clever. She'd have kept that sort of thing in some place where it was safe."

"Perhaps under the double bottom of a highboy in her bedroom, maybe," said Bryce.

"Double bottom?" Miss Ingham seemed mystified. "Am I telling you things you know already, Mr. Bryce?"

"Nope." Jim chuckled softly. "Have you told Johnson any of this?"

"Why, no. He didn't ask me," Miss Ingham returned.

Jim chuckled again. "Did Miss Kenton have a typewriter at her rooms, Miss Ingham?"

"Certainly," Miss Ingham said. "But why?"

"Because," Jim's expression was actually gloating, "I may want to examine it before we're done with this business, young woman."

"Before?" The woman smiled. "Then you're going into it for Bob?"

"Well—" Bryce said, "you might leave us your address, in case we need it. And tell O'Neil that we'll be over for a talk."

"I will." Miss Ingham rose and stood beside my desk. All at once her voice was unsteady and her mouth was tremulous. "You—see, I'm—in love with the big simpleton myself."

She dabbed at her eyes with a kerchief; then, hastily, she gave me her address, smiled again, and walked out.

BRYCE CLEARED his throat. "Speakin' of avocados, suppose you ask Johnson to join us for lunch. We'll take them notes with us.' I may be damp behind the ears, but I've got a hunch there was a hook-up between the Kenton frail and that gig."

I rang the station and arranged to meet Johnson at a cafe where we frequently lunched. He met us twenty minutes later, and we managed to get a table by ourselves.

"What's on your minds?" he asked, when our order was given.

"Mainly," said Jim, "that we're out to prove you put salt on the wrong bird's tail in that O'Neil arrest."

"Yeah?" Johnson's expression was noncommittal. "And so what?"

"We're workin' for him, since this mornin'," said Jim. "An' we want to talk to him this afternoon. It seemed polite to tell you."

"An' you're always polite!"

Johnson grinned.

He and Bryce always engaged in a rough and ready banter when they got together.

"Who dragged you in, guy?" Johnson demanded.

"Gladys Ingham," said Jim. "She gave us the low down on that Kenton dame. What would you say to her workin' a black-mailin' game?"

For a minute Johnson did not answer; then he grinned again. "I reckon nothing you could say would surprise me."

"Yeah. The trouble with you is there's such a lot of things you don't know," Bryce rejoined. "Listen, fella,"

He outlined the incident leading up to our presence in the Silver Moon the night before, and as he described them placed the notes in Johnson's hand.

Johnson read them.

"Don't sound so bad," he said when he was done. "If you'll let me have the one about Palloni I can maybe give you some help. We been checkin' on things at the Kenton woman's office, and I can have one of the boys from the identification bureau run it out."

"Okay," Bryce accepted on the instant. "I was hopin' you'd see it that way, without my askin'.—Now, here's something else for your consideration."

He went on to recount our interview with Palloni, our visit to Cerra's quarters and our conversation with Gladys Ingham.

"Holy smoke!" Johnson grumbled when Jim paused. "You sure are a helpful cuss. Here I have an A-one murder, with a likely suspect, and you spring a couple of squeeze *billets-doux* an' shoot the works."

Bryce grinned in understanding. "Yep. We're a coupla Boy Scouts. But it's as reasonable for the gig to have done it as for O'Neil to have gunned the girl who was plannin' to take him to Europe."

"I can see that myself," Johnson scowled. "I know the Jumpin' Jack an' the broad he lives with. But this is the first I've heard of these notes. Come along if you want to see O'Neil. Richfield was over to see him this morning."

"Goin' to defend him, is he?" I asked.

"Sure. Richfield's a clever mouthpiece. Let's get going," said Johnson, rising.

FIFTEEN MINUTES later, we were standing outside a cell in which Bob O'Neil sat in a posture of dejection. The guard let us in, and then left us.

"Good afternoon, O'Neil," I said. "We saw Miss Ingham this morning, and we've come over for a talk."

"I know. She told me you were coming." The fiancé of the late Margaret Kenton put out a hand. "But I'm afraid I can't tell you very much. The whole this is—like a nightmare. I can't seem to realize it—to realize that Marge is—gone." I saw the muscles harden in his jaws as he sought for emotional control.

"Perhaps, then," I said, "it would be better for us merely to ask for whatever information we deem essential, and let you answer as you can."

He paled, visibly.

"Why—yes." He nodded. "Sit down, won't you?"

We seated ourselves, Jim on a stool and I beside our client, on the gray prison blanket of his cot.

"Did you call at Miss Kenton's apartment before or after Miss Ingham and Torrance got there?" I began.

"Before," he said, without the slightest hesitation. "The elevator girl will tell you."

"And you were alone together, until they came."

"Yes." O'Neil paused for a moment. "I suppose you're thinking about that gun. I could have taken it, of course. But why should I? I loved Margaret. I meant to marry her. Good God—"

He broke off and sat breathing deeply.

"How long have you known her?" Jim inquired.

"A year, No—a trifle longer," O'Neil replied.

"And how well did you know her?" Jim questioned.

"Just what do you mean by that?" O'Neil demanded, glowering at him.

"What I say," Jim rejoined. "We're trying to fix the responsibility for what happened last night. Things like that don't happen without a reason. Now, do you know anything at all that might give us a little help?"

"Reason, eh?" O'Neil nodded. "But it's all so utterly without reason I We were sitting there in the night club, talking about our future plans. Then she asked me to get her bag, and I went to the check room and came back and found her—dead. I—" He checked himself and fought again for control. "It seems an unthinkable thing to say, but it's almost as though she had asked for her bag to get me out of the way. And if I'd stayed there—if I hadn't left her—"

"You were talkin' about your trip to Europe?" Jim suggested.

"Yes," O'Neil said dully. "Not that it matters—now. Did Gladys tell you?"

I nodded.

"POOR KID," he said. "She thinks she's partly to blame for my arrest. But that's foolish. My story simply fell down, after that doctor found Margaret's bag. I don't blame Inspector Johnson, of course."

"Was Miss Kenton expecting to receive a considerable sum of money?"

"Yes." He flushed. "From an estate. But—I wasn't marrying her for money. It was just that she felt we'd be foolish to wait, at our ages. You see, Marge would have been twenty-seven the twenty-eighth of next month."

"And how old are you?" said Bryce.

"I'll be twenty-nine on the eleventh," O'Neil replied. "But about this money. It made a difference. Life had been hard for Marge. She'd made her own way for nine years, first as a stenographer, then as a court reporter, then in Richfield's office, and then in a business of her own. But she'd always wanted to travel, and so for our honeymoon we planned a trip to Europe."

"How much cash was she expectin' to get?" said Jim.

"Somewhere around a half million," O'Neil told him.

"An'—was there any one else who mighta got it if she didn't?" Bryce frowned.

"Why—my God!" O'Neil's eyes widened and narrowed. "I don't know. I swear I don't. Marge merely said it was coming to her, and last night she said she expected it inside a week."

"She told you that while you were at the Moon, do you mean?"

"No—" O'Neil hesitated briefly. "At her rooms."

"Well, all right." Jim rose. "You sit tight, O'Neil, and don't talk to any one but us an' Richfield. He's your lawyer?"

"Yes," O'Neil assented. "He was Margaret's friend, and he came to see me this morning."

We took our leave.

"She was expectin' a half million inside a week, an' she tells him so at her rooms, last night," Jim said when we were outside the jail. "An' then she gets bumped off with her own cannon. Now does that make sense, I ask you? An' the answer is—it don't.—Let's ask Johnson if he's any objection to lettin' us go through the woman's rooms."

I agreed, and we made our way to the detective's office, to prefer our request and put the inspector in touch with the results of our interview.

He scribbled an admittance order to the officer on guard at Margaret Kenton's apartment.

"And it wouldn't do any harm for you to run off a line or two on a machine that I saw there last night," he said as he handed it to Jim. "I'd have done it myself, if I'd known about those notes at the time. If she wrote them, that's something to chew on, of course. But I'm a lot more interested in her havin' expected a wad of money from an estate."

"Meanin'?" Bryce said as he put the permit in his pocket.

"Meanin' that if she told O'Neil about the money, an' if there was some way of gettin' the jack without the woman, I wouldn't feel more than a million miles off in havin' grabbed that bird, last night," Inspector Johnson returned. "Five hundred grand is a lot of money, and she was killed with her own gat."

"Yeah." Jim took out a cigar and set it afire. "You find the mug that put a muffler on that cannon, and you'll have the man who gave her the works. If she was workin' a blackmailin' racket, it's just possible she overplayed her hand. Well—let us know what you dig up, willya?"

"Sure," Johnson agreed. "As long as that runs both ways. But why don't you take it up with Semi-Dual. It's beginnin' to look like his sort of case."

CHAPTER V

A CASE FOR SEMI-DUAL

SEMI-DUAL! BRIEFLY I had a mental picture of the man known as Semi-Dual—tall and of a commanding presence, leonine of head, gray-eyed, with a strongly bridged, aquiline nose. Semi-Dual, philosopher and modern metaphysician, who dwelt in the square white tower atop the building in which Bryce and I had our offices. Long before penthouses were the vogue, he had made that tower his abode; he had built a garden about it, with a sundial and a tiny fountain beside the flower-bordered path that led from the top of a bronze and marble stairway.

Semi-Dual—our friend. The man who had inspired our partnership from the first; who had been the "god in the machine" of our venture ever since; who had upon many a baffling case lent us the aid of his marvelous knowledge of life and its forces.

Johnson knew him also; had worked with him and with us on more than one occasion in the past. Hence I knew what he meant by saying that this was his sort of a case. Because—

In Dual's philosophy, material values had little place. But the spiritual values, as he called them, bulked very large. Life and its integrity, its rights both of bodily and of mental freedom, were things which he held sacred and which he was ready to defend at need. Priest of Justice, I sometimes called him to myself. For Justice was his creed.

Years spent in the study of the Universal Laws had given Semi-Dual a transcending understanding of Universal Force; he had acquired the ability to turn the laws at which the average

man is wont to scoff to his needs. As an example, astrology—
that study of the stars which was employed by the ancients long
before astronomy was evolved. For him, astrology was a thing
reduced to a practical basis; it was no more than a demonstra-
tion of the electro-magnetic force by which the very Universe
is balanced.

However, Dual was a practical person, in every sense of the
word. For although he gave full credence to the convictions
which he gained from his own abstruse calculations, he never
asked credence for another, unless he was in a position to furnish
concrete proof.

"Material proof for material man," he had said to me many a
time since I had known him.

Well, here was a case in which a man was under suspicion
of having murdered the woman whom he alleged he loved—a
case, past any doubt, in which what Dual called "spiritual values"
were the major issues.

As a result I was quite prepared for my partner's comment,
"Yeah. I been thinkin' of doin' that very thing ever since O'Neil
happened to mention the date of the Kenton dame's birth, and
since I asked him about his own. You know, that's the sort of
dope Semi always needs."

Johnson nodded. He knew Dual's methods.

"Then why don't you play the hunch?" he urged. "Here we
got four suspects—"

"FOUR?" SAID Jim.

"Sure. O'Neil, the Jumpin' Jack, the Ingham frail and Palloni.
Joe coulda framed it with the Jack—or that gorilla of his, Tovallo.
If, as the Ingham twist says, Cerra was in the habit of goin' to
her office, maybe he also went to her rooms. That way, he coulda
got her gun an' slipped it to Tovallo last night, when he went to
Joe's table just before that dance.

"Or the Ingham girl might have gunned her, after the dance,
an' dropped the gun an' screamed. She went back to their table
alone. That mug Torrance says he stopped to speak to a man

who owed him some money, an' since both of them were in the Kenton girl's flop before they came to the Moon, she could have easy got the gun. Besides, she's in love with O'Neil, an' she knew the other doll was planning to take him to Europe."

"Okay, except that the lights was up an' the music wasn't playin'," said Jim.

"An' she mighta counted on those very facts to make it look like it happened while she *was* with Torrance. Nobody was lookin' for such a thing.—But she could have done it in ten seconds." Johnson indulged in a sinister grin. "Anyway, it looks like the thing was up Dual's alley. Why don't you—"

"We're goin' to," Bryce clamped his cigar between his teeth in sudden determination. "Come along, old son!"

FIFTEEN MINUTES later we mounted the stairs from the twentieth floor of the Urania Building to Semi-Dual's garden, and stepped on a metal plate displaying a message in letters of colored glass:

> Pause and consider, oh, stranger. For he who cometh against me with evil intent shall live to rue it, until the uttermost part of his debt shall have been paid. Yet he who cometh in peace, and with a pure heart, shall surely find that which he seeketh.

It was actually an annunciator plate which waked a chime of bells in the tower. They rang now like temple bells as we went up the path to the door of the tower and found it open. Henri, Dual's sole servitor and companion, was bowing before us.

"Welcome, friends of the master."

"Bon jour, Henri," I returned, and passed him to cross an anteroom furnished in harmonizing tones of brown.

I rapped on a farther door.

"Come," the perfectly modulated voice of Semi-Dual replied.

We entered the room beyond, and Dual rose from beside a huge, flat-topped desk. I have named him a Priest of Justice, and there was a hint of the priest about him as he stood. As was his custom when alone, he was clad in a flowing robe of white, edged with purple on hem and sleeve. Above it, I met the glance of his gray eyes.

They were deep, those eyes of Semi-Dual—deep with the wisdom of wide experience, and calm as his own garden; yet they were lighted by an inner fire of the spirit so that at times there were tiny flecks of living light within them, suggesting the gleam from an open window through which the soul of the man looked forth.

At his back was an actual window. And at the end of his desk was a life-sized figure of Venus in bronze—an electro-lier from which light was shed from a golden apple held in an outstretched hand.

I noted it all as a familiar setting for the man who spoke in greeting:

"Welcome, my friends. Be seated, and speak to me of those things which give me once more the pleasure of your presence."

To the casual observer, the words might have seemed fulsome. But knowing him as I did, as the son of a Persian noble and a Russian petty princess, I found them no more than an expression of the blended bloods in his veins. And because I knew him, I told him our story from first to last, omitting no slightest detail, exactly as he himself had taught me to do in the past.

WHILE I spoke, he sat with lowered lids. One could have fancied him asleep. But I knew he was never more alive—that his mind was avidly reaching out to catch and judge every word. And the instant I came to the end of my tale he opened his eyes, drew a sheet of paper to him, and rapidly noted the dates of O'Neil's and Margaret Kenton's births.

"And now the note which is still in your possession?" he requested, taking it and reading it, and then laying it to one side. "A revealing missive," he declared, "inasmuch as it mirrors the personality of the writer. One may assume the author to be an individual of an inherent criminal bent. If, as you assume, the woman Margaret Kenton devised this screed, of obvious purpose, then I would say that Margaret Kenton was a woman of criminal inclination—in financial matters, at least."

"And you think a woman wrote it?"

"Yes," Dual replied. "I presume you know nothing more of the girl than you have told me?"

"Not yet." I shook my head.

"Learn all you may," Dual advised. "As a man soweth, so shall he reap. And the sum of his acts, be they good or bad, is no more than a balance set up in the Ledger of Life, which, in the final equation, must determine whether he shall stand or fall. And in this woman's life we may find the reason why she died.—If the Ingham woman is really in love with O'Neil, she will scarcely refuse to aid you in his behalf."

"Unless Johnson is right in thinking that she did it herself," said Bryce.

Dual considered. "Were Johnson correct, what could her crime avail her, if through it she finds the life of the man imperiled?" he rejoined at length. "Women in love, my friends, are prone to sacrifice."

The speech was characteristic. Dual was slow to accuse or judge. Words, to him, were things to be carefully used—intangible psychic swords that could injure the one against whom turned. We both knew his attitude.

"WELL, I'M no psychologist," Bryce remarked as Semi paused. "But we ain't overlookin' the Ingham filly, an' we're goin' through the Kenton girl's rooms tonight."

"Also, confer with the attorney, Richfield," said Semi-Dual. "If he is to defend O'Neil, he should be willing to tell you something concerning the murdered woman's life. Some moments ago I spoke of indicative straws. Go gather them, my friends— those fractional integers of meaning so important at times to the final balance of the Cosmic Ledger. I shall erect the astral charts of O'Neil and the Kenton woman."

"Speakin' of straws," Jim said as we descended from the garden, "let's ring up Richfield an' see if we can see him."

I glanced at my watch. It was after three.

"All right," I assented.

We returned to the office, to find that Johnson had called while we were out. I rang him up at the station and found satisfaction in his voice.

"Well, I reckon we're all hooked up. That note you gave me was wrote in the Kenton girl's office, accordin' to our boys. Of course the thing's lousy with the Martin frill's fingerprints and Palloni's, and yours too. But—there's one you didn't manage to smudge, an' it's the Kenton woman's. That signs an' seals it, because it matches the prints we took since she was cooled.—Seen Dual?"

"Yes," I said. "And we're going to see Richfield if we can, and to-night we're going through that blackmailer's flop."

"Well, say," he offered a suggestion, "drop by the station about eight and I'll go with you."

"Right," I agreed, and called Richfield's office.

Dan rapped, and came in as I was putting the receiver back in its cradle.

"Say, listen," he announced. "That red-headed twist is outside, waitin' to see you."

"Okay," said Bryce. "Let her come in."

"Good afternoon!" Miss Ingham said as she appeared. "Have you seen Inspector Johnson since I was here this morning?"

"Why, yes," I returned, arrested by her palpably nervous manner.

"Did he say anything about me?"

Her eyes met mine and I found her pupils abnormally large.

CHAPTER VI

IN THE EVENT OF DEATH

"**JUST WHAT DO** you think Inspector Johnson might have said about you?" Bryce asked.

Gladys Ingham breathed deeply before she answered. "I don't know. But—about last night. Dick—I mean Mr. Torrance and I talked it over today at lunch—"

"Are you referring to the fact that Torrance wasn't with you when you discovered Miss Kenton dead?" I interrupted.

"Yes." Miss Ingham nodded.

"An' was your friend Torrance afraid that Johnson might think you gunned her yourself after you got back to your table?" asked Jim.

The woman paled before so direct an attack. Her lids half closed.

"It's—almost obvious, isn't it?" she finally said, and went on in a voice which gained by degrees in force. "There was opportunity enough, I suppose. But—I can't help how it looks. I didn't do it. I'm—just not that sort. God knows I had reason enough to hate her and the coldblooded way in which she practically—bought Bob."

"Bought him?" I repeated, aware of an unpleasant reaction to her words. "Do you mean O'Neil didn't really love her?"

"No—I don't mean that," Miss Ingham returned. "That was the pity of it; he did. I've already told you he was simple-minded. What I mean is that if she hadn't been expecting a fortune, she couldn't have planned a trip to Europe, and he might have had time to find out what she was."

"A blackmailin' biddy?" said Bryce.

Miss Ingham eyed him. "I don't know. Was she really?"

"Sure." Bryce made no effort at evasion.

The woman set her lips. "Then—she was even worse than I thought. Have you any proof? Something she'd written on one of her machines—or something you found in that drawer with the double bottom?"

"You're a bright girl." Jim smiled.

"Scarcely that, I'm afraid." Miss Ingham shook her head. "But I'm bright enough to know that Bob would never have looked at her twice if he'd suspected. And now you've told me how she was getting her money, I'm wondering if her story about an inheritance was true—or if she was expecting—"

"To get it by blackmail, eh?" Bryce grinned. "I've trifled with that thought myself."

"Yes, I suppose so." All at once the girl's voice seemed tired. "You've thought of pretty much everything. But if she was trying to get it by—extortion—might that it not explain—?"

"Five hundred grand is a lot of money," Bryce cut in.

Miss Ingham nodded. "I suppose so," she said. "I'm wasting your time. And I can't help what your friend the Inspector thinks. I didn't kill Marge.—But do what you can for Bob."

"We'll do all we can," I assured her. "And what we need now is all the information concerning Miss Kenton that we can obtain. If you worked for her and went to night clubs with her—"

"OH, BUT"—SHE cut me off, with a tinge of color in face and throat—" that was because of Bob. And I think she knew it, and asked me to go along because she knew it. She was cruel, Mr. Glace. She knew too many things. You know, she was once a court reporter and she picked up a lot of nasty tricks."

Death's wing brushed the police car.

"We'll probably dig up the dirt on her as we go along," Bryce said.

Miss Ingham reverted to her former topic. "But what does Inspector Johnson think about me?"

"Nothin' definite," Jim countered bluntly. "Right now, we're gatherin' straws. We ain't ready to make bricks.—An' we never will be, unless we get to work." He drew out his watch in a pointed manner.

Miss Ingham took the hint. "Then I mustn't detain you. Good-afternoon, Mr. Glace."

"And that," Jim declared, when the door had closed behind her, "oughta put me in my place. It looks like Johnson has got that baby worried. And when they're worried is when they slip. But she sure hated Kenton!—Let's keep that date with Rich-field."

O'Neil's attorney received us in a well-appointed room where a slender vase on a polished desk contained a single exqui-site rose. There was an exquisiteness, too, in the iron gray hair brushed back from his colorless, well bred face and forehead; in the meticulous detail of his grooming, so complete as to barely escape a hint of foppishness.

But there was nothing of foppishness in the cold, blue glance he turned upon us.

"Really, gentlemen, I'm inclined to feel that you're wasting your time as well as mine," he said. "If, as you say, you are working for O'Neil, I shall cooperate, of course. But you must remember that I was Miss Kenton's friend rather than his; and I can think of little that will be of help to you in your investigations. May I ask you to be brief?"

"Brief as possible," I returned. "As it happens, it is about Miss Kenton we want to see you. As her former employer, have you ever heard or known of anything that might cause you to think of her as one who would practice blackmail?"

He frowned, and fiddled with a paper knife before he probed my purpose.

"Just what is behind that question, Mr. Glace?" he demanded.

I told him, and he listened without comment.

"**I THINK** you shock me," he said, when at length I paused. "Margaret was in my office for over two years, and I found her most efficient. I met her when she was a court reporter, on a case heard in chambers."

"Dirty?" Bryce asked.

Richfield gave him a glance.

"None too savory," he answered. "Are you suggesting that she may have obtained information which she later employed to her monetary gain, from such or similar sources?"

"Well—seein' that cases heard in chambers are often pretty juicy, maybe I was," Jim replied.

"I see." Richfield frowned again. "What I started to say, however, was that her work in this particular case attracted my attention, and that later I took her into my office."

"And why did she leave?" Jim inquired.

"Not that it concerns you, but her purpose was to organize

her own business," Richfield returned, in a tone of what seemed to be annoyance.

"No other reason?" Bryce questioned, baldly.

"None," Richfield actually snapped. "But in case you retain any doubt, let me add that even after she left, I occasionally took to her bits of particular work, work of a technical nature.— Because of the fact that she understood as well my requirements."

"Did you know she intended to marry O'Neil?" Bryce asked.

"Certainly. She told me," Richfield assented, and went on: "To me, the whole—er—tragic occurrence smacks of the bizarre. She was alive, before the last dance, because I caught her eye and she acknowledged my salutation. Yet at the end of that dance, her life was blotted out.—And now comes this story of blackmail. Gentlemen, I am amazed! Did the police discover anything beyond the fact that the notes were written in her office?"

"Not that we've heard about," Bryce declared.

"And the machine falls short of conclusive evidence, of course."

"Meanin' that somebody else mighta used it?" Jim suggested. "It's her fingerprint that ties it up, of course."

Richfield narrowed his lids. "Yet one might think that if she were making a business of it, she might have left some other evidence."

"An' I ain't sayin' she didn't—or that some joker didn't beat us to it," Bryce rejoined.

"How do you mean?" Richfield's tone was startled.

Bryce explained concerning the drawer with the double bottom in the dead girl's rooms, and went on, "But there's just a chance that we've got a lead on that. At the Silver Moon there's a gig by the name of Giovanni Cerra. We think he was workin' with her. An' if he was, an' knew she was dead—"

"He might have entered her room before Johnson posted a guard," Richfield interrupted. "Is that it, Mr. Bryce?"

"Well," Jim grinned. "I don't reckon he did it afterwards."

For the third time, Richfield scowled.

"Margaret died at eleven-ten, or close to it," he said in the tone of a man who thinks aloud. "I left the Moon at a little after twelve. Yes—there would have been time, I imagine.—Why did Johnson lock the door after the horse was stolen?"

"There wasn't any reason to think there was a horse, at first," Bryce said a trifle stiffly. "Or that somebody'd search her flop the minute she was cooled. Who'd you have in mind, just now, when you said there might have been time."

SUDDENLY RICHFIELD smiled. "You're a literal person, aren't you, Bryce? I had no one in mind, unless it was the man you mentioned, of course. I merely meant he could have done it between the time Margaret was shot and the time Johnson posted his guard."

"And that," I said, "would mean that whoever did it knew she was dead, or would be, and hence was either in the cafe or entered her rooms after she left them, with the advance knowledge that she wasn't coming back."

"Holy pickled herring!" Bryce exclaimed. "Remember what that Martin pullet told us Palloni said about that note? That may have been baloney—"

"Just a minute," Richfield stayed his outburst. "May I ask what you're talking about? Do you mean that Palloni, the—er—gangster?"

"Sure." Jim chuckled and explained at considerable length. "Honest, Mr. Richfield, we don't know anything, really. We're just gatherin' straws, in the hope that one of 'em may break some camel's back. Up to now, though, we've got darned few straws—'an' not a single camel, outside of O'Neil, an' he looks like a goat."

"And one of your suppositions," Richfield said, "is that Margaret may have run counter to some of this—er—gangster's plans?—You still feel that her death was murder?"

"Don't you?" said Jim.

"No." The lawyer shook his head. "Let us look at facts. She is killed with her own gun. It lay at her feet—and the cloth of her gown was scorched by the discharge. Furthermore, it appears, as I have learned to-day, that she had actually prepared for the eventuality of her death."

"What's that?" Bryce literally exploded, while I felt a chill sensation run down my back. "Prepared for it how, Mr. Richfield?"

"She had made a will," the lawyer said, with a faint smile twitching his mouth. "And although I have not as yet seen it, according to my client the document names him as heir to all her possessions at the time of her death."

CHAPTER VII

DEATH'S WING

AT ANOTHER TIME, I might have laughed at Bryce. He not only stared; he gaped. And I found myself no less constrained to a startled silence by Richfield's words. I saw their possible implication. I recalled that Johnson had said a few hours before that had it been possible for O'Neil to obtain the money without the woman, he would be satisfied with his arrest. Now O'Neil was her heir!

"He—told you that when you was over to see him this morning?"

"Yes, Mr. Bryce." The lawyer's voice was precise. "And he gave me written authority to take charge of her affairs, in his behalf."

I shook myself together. "She made the will recently?" I asked.

"That is a pertinent question," Richfield replied. "And one which supports my view of the case. O'Neil says she executed the document three days ago, and placed it in a safety deposit box—which I will have opened after due formalities, of course. The knowledge surprised me, I confess. But she was madly in love, I imagine. Romance came late into her life. I have heard her laugh at the weaknesses and frailties it so often masks.

"She was an orphan—had made her own way unaided. I know that she made money through, as she claimed, investments. That is a claim which your suggestion of blackmail may possibly cloud. In either case, it appears that she wanted O'Neil to have whatever she left. As affecting O'Neil right now, the thing is rather a two-edged sword. But if we can establish his love for her in the minds of the jury, it will become a weapon in defense of his innocence. And if we show her engaged in blackmail, we shall be able to widen the field of suspicion."

"And when are you takin' charge of her affairs?" Jim asked.

"At once," Richfield told him. "I made arrangements for her burial this afternoon.—I shall also do what I can to free O'Neil from all suspicion."

For the first time I noted a surge of human emotion in his tone. Then it was gone, and he was the coldly analytical lawyer again.

"I expect to spend a part of this evening at her rooms, provided I can arrange the matter with the police."

"I reckon you can." Bryce grinned. "We were thinking of going through them ourselves. If you like, we'll take you along."

"I certainly would," Richfield accepted. "I'll meet you at the Willden at any time you name."

"Around eight," Jim suggested and rose.

And that was the situation, less than twenty-four hours after Margaret Kenton had been shot to death in the Silver Moon.

"WHEW!" BRYCE broke into comment as we reached the street. "For just a minute after Richfield said that doll had left a will in O'Neil's favor, you coulda fanned me down with a feather. I'd sure like to know whether the Ingham twist knew anything about it."

"You're not suggesting that she may have thought she could win both the man and the money, are you?" I demanded.

"I ain't suggestin' nothin'," he returned. "I'm just huntin' straws.—Say, Hendricks's place is up here about a block. Let's drop in an' tell him he can stop worryin' about the widow. To-morrow you can drop the Martin kid a line to run in and get her note. I'll get it off Johnson to-night."

That Hendricks was relieved, no one could doubt.

"I knew the girl. We've done business for her," he said. "And

I read about her death. But I never thought it had a bearing in my direction. Thanks, Jim. If you'll send me a bill, I'll see that you get a check."

"And now," Bryce proposed when we had left the broker's office, "let's get hold of Johnson and slip him the low-down while we eat."

Johnson, however, surprised us both when we had put him in possession of the facts.

"Now that I've got it, I don't know that I want it," he said in a well nigh musing tone. "The thing's infernally clever. It looks crazy—but it ain't. Anybody coulda plugged her an' dropped the gun an' walked off.

"Damn it, I wish I could hang it on Palloni. There's one guy I'd love to knock over! We've come to a helluva pass in this country, when a wolf like him can run at large. There ain't a doubt he'd have shoved her off if she got in his way. And I reckon he knew her racket, all right. But somehow it ain't like his work. He'd have been more apt to take her for a ride and dump her in the bushes.—As for the gig, we got a tail on him, of course."

"Too bad you didn't have one on him last night," said Bryce. "If you had, we might know what was in the drawer with the double bottom—"

"Yeah!" Johnson cut him short. "The next thing, you'll be suggestin' that the Jumpin' Jack is plannin' to carry on the business."

"And he might, at that," Jim agreed. "He's seen it work. I wonder if he slipped her Hendricks's five yards, before they gave her the works."

"It wasn't on her, after the shootin'." Johnson drew his watch. "If we're to meet that mouthpiece, let's get movin'. I got a car outside."

But though his words were casual, what followed was anything but that.

WE ENTERED the police machine, and Johnson directed the chauffeur to the Willden. We shot away from the curb, and five minutes later we reached the foot of a curving viaduct—a roadway flung across a deep ravine, above a lower driveway that threaded the sylvan beauty of one of the city's parks. It was then that Death brushed us with his wing.

From the rear, a car came toward us—a dark car running without lights. In a roaring rush it was upon us, was veering toward us, forcing us to the side. I heard Johnson shout a raucous warning. And then came a grinding jar, the lurch of our machine to the ramming contact of the other, a sickening plunge, and a crash.

I heard the rail of the viaduct splinter with a rending metallic sound. I felt our car sag drunkenly on the edge of the abyss, then catch and hang there, the nose and the front wheels over, the rear still holding to the road, as it seemed to me then, by the weight of our bodies alone.

"God!" I heard Johnson gasp. Then he spoke to the chauffeur, bent forward over the wheel. "Jerry!—Hey, Jerry! You all right?"

No answer. The driver neither spoke nor moved. And the other car had fled away into the night.

Then, in the glow of the dash lamp, I saw a part of the viaduct railing, projecting in a twisted and sinister suggestion through the front of our machine. It had been driven through the chauffeur's body like a deadly spear, and I felt myself sicken at the sight.

"Hey—Jerry!" Johnson called again, and reached for the unconscious man.

The car tilted dizzily with his movement, and Bryce dragged him back.

"Sit still or you'll have us all over!" he admonished harshly. "They meant to put us over. Don't you get it?"

"Never mind that now," Johnson snarled. "We got to get Jerry off that wheel."

"Then let Gordon do it. He's married, an' we ain't," said Jim. "He can get out an' see what he can do, while we keep this bus balanced."

Even then, I felt an admiration for the man.

Johnson gave instant assent. "That's right, Glace. Get out and do what you can."

By that time, however, there was help at hand. Cars had come up and stopped at sight of our predicament. There were many hands. They steadied the car while we dragged Jerry out.

His face was covered with blood from a cut in his scalp which another piece of the rail had made when it tore through the front of our machine.

Johnson, quite himself again, took charge at once. He sent a volunteer to telephone for help, applied a first aid bandage to Jerry's head, and sent him off in another car. And then the three of us waited until a wrecking car and another police machine appeared.

Five minutes later, we were on our way to the Willden once more, and Bryce was speaking.

"Well that's that, but if you ask me, I wouldn't care to try it again! And there's one thing certain—somebody knows a lot more about what we're doing than we do. They meant to put us over. I tell you, the thing was planned."

"Yeah, it was," said Johnson, and his tone was grim.

CHAPTER VIII

CLUE CHASE

THE WILLDEN WAS little different from a hundred other buildings of its kind. We went in and finding no sign of Richfield, approached an elevator cage. On the seventh floor Johnson led the way to the door of a suite and rapped.

"Evenin', Hansen," he spoke to the man who opened, and paused at sight of Richfield seated beyond the guard. "Hello, Mr. Richfield," he said. "We're late, but somebody tried to ram us off the park viaduct just now, an' it all took time."

"No harm done, apparently." Richfield waved a hand. "Allow me to compliment you on the discipline of your man. When you didn't arrive, I waited awhile, and then came up. But he's played watch dog on me ever since."

"Mr. Richfield is taking charge, Hansen," Johnson said. "You can give him the key and report at the station."

"Okay, sir."

The policeman grinned and handed the key to the lawyer.

I glanced around. There was a living room, a bedroom, a kitchenette and a bath in the apartment.

Hansen went out, and Johnson glanced at the lawyer. "And now, if you like, I'll show you that drawer with the double bottom."

He entered the bedroom, and we followed.

"Here it is," he said, and stooped before an old fashioned highboy, to pull out the lower drawer. I saw that its contents were bits of intimate feminine apparel in a jumbled mass of color.

"Everything mussed up like this last night, or did you do it?" I suggested.

"Nope. They was just about like this," Johnson told me.

Everything else in the bedroom was in order. I nodded, went down on my knees, and began lifting out clinging bits of crepe and silk and satin.

"What do you expect that to get you?" Johnson growled.

I shook my head and continued my examination. Bryce bent beside me. Richfield smoked on a chair.

Then I took up a bit of crepe, and paused at sight of a small irregular hole, the edges of which were scorched!

"Maybe it's this," I said and held it up.

"Spark from a cigarette, most likely," Bryce volunteered a possible explanation.

"The girl smoke?" Johnson turned to Richfield.

"Oh, yes." The attorney nodded.

"Then I don't reckon it amounts to much," Johnson said. "She coulda done it any time she was sittin' around in the thing—say before goin' to bed, or while she was makin' up."

"Except that it hasn't been worn since it was burned," I pointed out.

"Huh?" Bryce caught at my meaning. "And that might mean it was burned while somebody smokin' a cigarette was goin' through this drawer.—Say, Mr. Richfield, what brand did Miss Kenton smoke?"

"Why, I don't know. Is it important?" Richfield appeared to be amused. "Would the brand make any difference in the hole?"

"Maybe not." Bryce frowned. "But there's an ash tray on a stand in the other room, an' it's full of butts."

JOHNSON CHUCKLED. "And you was thinkin' whoever burned a hole in her undies mighta left whatever he was smokin'.—You always was a broadminded thinker, Jim. I don't reckon—"

"An' you wasn't asked to," Bryce cut him off. "*You* ain't found a thing except a double-bottomed drawer with nothing in it."

"Gentlemen—gentlemen!" Richfield interposed. "Must you quarrel over your clues? There were four people here last evening—possibly five. Assuming that each of them smoked, Mr. Bryce will probably find several different brands in that ash tray, if he cares to take a look while you complete your examination of the *empty* drawer."

"Okay." Johnson drew the drawer completely out of the highboy while Bryce left the room. "Here's what put us wise," he said, indicating a discrepancy between the actual depth and the position of the visible bottom. "Now wait."

He produced a pocket knife and pried up the carefully fitted upper layer of wood.

"And there you are! Empty as an unkept promise."

"Just so," Richfield agreed, rising. "And now let's see what Bryce has found."

Johnson grinned, and thrust the crumpled garments back into the drawer, shoving the latter into place before he walked to the bedroom door.

"What luck with the snipe hunt, Jim?" he asked.

Bryce stood beside a smoker's stand on which he had arranged the stubs of a number of cigarettes. "Two toasted, two ships of the desert, six of a satisfyin' nature, an'—one of this here now nonchalant sort," he returned. "There's lipstick on the first, an' on some of the third, but none on the others."

"And where was the—er—nonchalant one in position to the others?" Richfield asked.

"Why," Bryce said as he gave him a glance, "it was nonchalantly shoved down on top of the rest."

"And would that mean it might have been deposited last?" the attorney said.

"I reckon I getcha," Jim rejoined. "Did whoever burned that hole in that crepe thing Glace discovered jam just that one stub into the tray before he left? He might have, at that, because you can see the end was rubbed some, to grind it out."

"And now all we gotta do is find somebody who nonchalantly grinds out that brand of smokes, to get our claws on the mug that went through this dump last night," Johnson grumbled. "Ain't *that* a lotta help?"

Richfield faced him in a manner of impatience.

"Almost, inspector. At last you have voiced an intelligent remark.—Four people were in this room. There is evidence that three other brands of cigarettes were smoked. Two bear stains of lipstick. We may assume that O'Neil and Miss Kenton smoked the same brand for—er—sentimental reasons; that Miss Ingham used the second paste-stained lot; and that Torrance smoked the others. Do you see the point?"

"I reckon O'Neil could tell you," Johnson replied, with none too good grace.

Richfield suddenly smiled. "Then suppose you find out.— And let's complete our work. If any one actually came here last night, I'd like to know why and who he was."

At the end, his smile was gone and his eyes were cold.

"You and us both," said Johnson. "Hop to it, boys!"

We finished our task. But not till I came to a spindle-legged writing desk with a folding top did we gain the least result. Then, from a pigeonhole, I drew a small morocco-bound memorandum book, and found it partly filled with columns of letters and numbers, connected by hyphens.

"Code, do you reckon?" Bryce suggested at my elbow.

"Pardon me, will you?"

Richfield took the hook from my fingers, studied it through a minute of silence, and gave it back.

"It appears," he said, "to be but another example of how a man who for years has rubbed shoulders with every stripe and caliber of human nature may be deceived. Margaret Kenton has proved the most bitter surprise of my life. And each new development, as it occurs, but serves to reveal her as a person who missed very little which she could—er—capitalize."

CHAPTER IX

THE DEBIT SIDE

"**THEN YOU KNOW** what it is?" Bryce spoke, referring to the book.

Richfield nodded. "In my estimation, it is no more than a record of legal cases. The letters and numbers serve to indicate the nature of the action."

"And it ought to be easy to prove," said Jim. "Any objection to our keeping it long enough to check up?"

"I'd be glad if you would," Richfield assented. "At present, she would appear to have invited her fate."

"Sort of gone into the red on the Ledger of Life, eh Jim made comment.

"Did O'Neil tell you anything specific concerning Miss Kenton's will?" I asked Richfield.

"Nothing specific," he returned. "Just why do you ask?"

"To discover the identity of the witness, or witnesses," I said.

"I see." He admitted the point. "But I understood that it was merely a line or two, naming him as heir, to act without bond. That is legal, so long as the will is entirely in her handwriting, and dated."

"And was it O'Neil's notion or hers?" Johnson growled.

"Hers, I imagine," Richfield told him. "O'Neil says he asked her why she wanted to draw it, and she merely laughed and said she wanted to feel sure that he would receive whatever was hers, in case anything happened to her."

"But that's *his* story," Johnson scowled.

Richfield's thin lips twitched. "I quite understand the several aspects of the matter, inspector. But if true, the statement would prove that her death, whether self-inflicted or not, was less a surprise to her than to any one else."

"You still pullin' the suicide line?" Johnson grumbled.

"Oh—I'm not pulling any line." Richfield shrugged. "But assuming that she was contemplating self-destruction, her actions were logical enough."

"Was they?" Johnson rasped. "She was expectin' to get a fortune an' marry O'Neil an' go to Europe."

"Speakin' of safety deposit boxes, maybe she kept her social dirt in one of them. Have you looked into that, Mr. Richfield?" Bryce interrupted.

"Not as yet." Richfield shook his head. "But assuming that these rooms were entered last evening, did you or did you not check up with the employees, inspector?"

"I did," Johnson responded gruffly. "I pulled all the kindergarten stuff. And there ain't any fingerprints, either. Let's get outa here. Bring your snipes if you want to, Bryce.

"And to-morrow," he said when Richfield had driven away in his car and we were on our way back to the station, "you two check up on that book Glace found. This dame Knew she was in some sort of danger.—How'd you put it, Bryce?"

His brows were knitted in the effort to recall.

"**GONE INTO** the red on the Ledger of Life, d'ye mean?" Jim said. "Semi-Dual pulled that to-day. You know, he thinks everything a man does adds up like a column of figures."

"Uh-huh," Johnson grunted. "An' I don't know but he's right. In my time, I've seen enough to make it practically certain that there's some sort of Bookkeeper on the job, and a mighty efficient one, too. By the way, I checked up on what Torrance said about speakin' to a guy at the Moon, while the Ingham girl went back to their table, an' it's straight. I tell you, this thing's deep.

"Take to-night. Somebody tried to gang us; but we're here

right now—just because they didn't hit us quite hard enough. An' *why* didn't they hit us as hard as they meant? Maybe Dual could tell us. Anyway, I'd like to know what he says."

"Well, then, let's go up now and see him," said Bryce. "It ain't so late."

Johnson gave the order. The car swerved, and presently came to a stand before the entrance to the Urania. We went in and took the elevator.

Dual's garden lay in shadow, when we reached it, soundless save for the splash of the tiny fountain, and lightless save for a yellow gleam in a window to tell us he was still awake. The tower chimes rang softly, and the tower door swung open and Henri bowed.

"You come quickly, again," he said. "But the Master does not sleep."

He bowed again, deferentially.

From the door beyond him, Dual spoke.

"Enter, my friends, and bring me the fruits of your searching."

We entered the room where the mellow light from the hand of the bronze Venus was cast on the desk in front of which he sat, with a mass of symbol-marked papers before him, the sign, manual of his work.

"Frankly," I said as we seated ourselves, "I don't know whether we bring you wheat or chaff. But you, I hope, have learned something."

"Of which," he returned, "I hold no proof save in the intangible indications thrown off by the Wheel in its turning, which with the man of to-day have small weight. Tell me, therefore, of your striving—if perchance we may thereby establish my less material findings, on a basis of determined fact."

I complied, and when I had finished, he sat for a time as a judge might sit to review a mass of evidence.

"**DEATH PASSED** close to you, my friends," he said at last. "But it was not written, as I knew, who have erected the charts of your lives in the past. For the rest, we are faced by a double triad—in this matter—the first being Mercury, Saturn and Neptune; the second Saturn, Mercury and Mars. A damnable quality appears. Neptune I see as Margaret Kenton, a woman dragged down, degraded, destroyed in a trap of her own contriving.

"Neptune normally rules the higher aspects of that which men call love. But Neptune, deprived of its normal octave of expression, may sink to abysmal depths. What you tell me of this woman is enough. She scoffed at love, and we have reason to feel that she dealt of deliberate purpose in its frankly animal phases of expression—to a sordid enrichment of herself.

"Yet, as in sex, there are ever dual factors, so there is a dual quality in the scheme of the Universe. Male and female, positive and negative, are but names for the two opposing forces through which that Universe exists. And therein was she tricked. Enriched by unclean knowledge, she in the end became the victim of the thing she had defiled."

"Meanin' she fell in love with O'Neil?" said Bryce.

"O'Neil, as I see it," said Semi-Dual, "was her downfall, and her God. Love, when it came to her at last, left her naked in her own eyes. She became afraid, I think, that he might discover her sordid story, and she sought a way of escape."

"By draggin' him off to Europe," Johnson suggested.

"Possibly," Dual replied. "She was secretive by nature. She had sold silence for a price. She was coldly calculating, and selfish. While Neptune appears to have prostituted her talents to a crafty seeking of material advantage, Mars shows in my horary figure as a selfish person."

"Her an' the Jumpin' Jack—" Jim began.

"Giovanni Cerra?" Dual checked him. "But Cerra, my friend, has wings on his feet, in the figure I have erected—Mercury, you know, was the messenger of the gods, and wore wings on his feet."

"Messenger, huh?" Bryce grinned. "Well, that ain't so bad. He picked up Hendricks's five yards—"

"Messenger of the gods," Semi-Dual corrected. "Their mills grind slowly exceeding fine. Perchance he will serve them yet, in the matter of their grist!"

HIS EYES met mine, and I found them flecked with those tiny points of light, as though his soul looked out of a window. And as always when I saw them, they gave me the impression of a purpose as implacable as fate—of an unemotional knowledge based on the interplay of the unescapable forces which shuttle endlessly to and fro between the stars. Life, Death—what did they matter, I thought. I quoted Omar aloud.

> *"We are no other than a moving row*
> *Of Magic Shadow-shapes that come and go*
> *Round with the Sun-illumined Lantern held*
> *In Midnight by the Master of the Show."*

"Aye!" Once more Dual smiled.

Johnson cleared his throat.

"But what about Cerra?" he questioned.

"Cerra," said Semi-Dual, "should be watched. I would like a more intimate knowledge of him. Is he of American or foreign birth? If the latter, the records should give us information as to his birth date, which I could use."

"If the records show, I'll get it for you," Johnson promised. "An' I got a question I wanta ask you flat. Was I right in pinchin' O'Neil or not?"

His query surprised me. He should have known better, I thought. Dual was not one to voice so definite an opinion, unless prepared to back it with proof. Even so, the point now so directly presented to him seemed difficult to evade. I saw Bryce purse his lips as we waited for the answer. It came:

"Eminently right, inspector. For by it you have knit the threads of the matter together; have brought justice into the equation, and directed the light of the sun upon the problem to the end that justice shall be served."

The words were characteristic of the man in the white and purple robes—as cryptic as he was wont to be until he was ready to speak.

Jim caught at its tag in characteristic fashion.

"The sun, huh? Just where does the sun come into this muddle?"

"As the symbol of the force and power of justice," Dual returned. "Hence the forces of law and order—the police—may stand for us who are allied with them to a common purpose in our ultimate success."

"Ultimate?" said Jim. "That sounds as though you were seein' a lot more to it than we do yet."

Dual made no immediate response. He merely sat at the desk whereon were the symbol-marked sheets from which he read the marches of the stars. But to me it seemed that knowledge sat there with him—as sure yet as remote as the pin-points of light that wheeled above us.

"And if I should tell you I felt assured of far more than I have said?" he returned at length.

"I'd believe you," Bryce declared, without hesitation.

For the third time, Dual smiled.

"Aye," he agreed. "One believes a thing he has oft seen proved. Today I said I would seek a balance in the Cosmic Ledger. That balance I have struck, and in it a debtor to Life stands forth. And if a debt there be, that debt shall be paid in one way or another. So, and so only, is the Cosmic Balance kept. There is nothing of chance in the equation.

"Observe how the progression moves. A woman is killed with an explosive weapon. A man goes to jail with explosive suddenness. We have in our possession a possible motive for the woman's death. Is this an accident? Nay. It is simply cause and effect; it is the grinding of the Mill, my friends.—Go, then, with, that assurance, and bring to the Mill whatever you find of—grist...."

"Back from the stars to Earth," Jim remarked as we left the Urania entrance. "I'm takin' my own advice an' huntin' a bed."

I found my car and dropped him at his quarters and drove home.

QUINN BARGED into my office at ten o'clock, the next morning, and flopped himself into a chair. "Get Mr. Jim in here, willya?" he said, an undisguised eagerness in face and voice.

I pressed a buzzer that brought Bryce to us.

"And now what have you stubbed your toe on?" I prompted.

Danny grinned. "Why, I know what became of the long end of Hendricks's five yards. The Jumpin' Jack blew it on a ring for that li'l blond broad of his."

"BEHAVE, BEHAVE," said Jim, with suddenly narrowed lids.

"How do you know he did?"

"Why, you see it was like this," Dan told him. "After I spoke of checkin' up on that rat, I got to thinkin' I might as well get busy right off the bat. So I ankled down to his flop in the afternoon an' hung around. The very first crack, I bump into a dick I know.

" 'Hello,' I says. 'Whatcha doin'?' An' he says, 'Tailing a gorilla Johnson wanted watched.' I asks him who, an' blessed if he didn't say the Jumpin' Jack. So I asks is he in his flop, an' this guy says he is. So we hung around, and after a bit here comes the rat an' his floosie. An' they walk down to Goldberg's an' go inside."

"The jewelers?" said Bryce.

"Sure." Dan nodded. "I tell Carrigan to wait, an' I ankle past. I see 'em inside; so I go back, an' it ain't long till they come out. The moil's got her left glove off an' is lookin' at her finger, smilin' at the rat. That was just before six. I tell Carrigan to tail 'em, an' I go in the store an' ask if they've sold this girl a ring, an' they say they have. They say the rat paid for it with four one-hundred-dollar bills.

"That sounds hot to me, an' I get the serial numbers. Then this mornin' I go down an' ask Hendricks to let me check 'em. An' that cinched it. The gig never even turned 'em over to the Kenton doll. What he does is blow four of 'em on a bit of ice. I go back an' pick up Carrigan, near the Moon, an' he says the gig an' the doll have gone inside. So I blow in an' the Jack an' his doll are eatin' at a table, an' I get chummy with a cigarette girl.

" 'Ain't that the kid what leads the show, over there at the Moon with the Jumpin' Jack?' I asks, an' she says, 'Sure.'—'What's her name?' I says. " 'Well,' she tells me, 'she calls herself Violet deLisle, but her real name's Maud Slade.'—'You love her, don't you?' I says. 'Like carbolic acid,' she pipes. 'But the Jack falls for her, all right. He's been promisin' her a ring for at least six months; an' believe it or not, to-day he makes good with a two-carat hunk of ice.'

" 'Where'd a gig get all that money?' I asks her. She gives her lips a sort of free-wheelin' motion. 'Oh, there's a lot of these fat mammas who like their papas young an' slender,' she says. 'Say—I ain't one of the entertainers. Do you want some cigarettes or not?'—So I buy a pack, an'—that's all, I guess, except that the gig can't be hep to the fact he's bein' tailed, or he'd never have fed those bills to Goldberg, less'n two days after the Kenton twist was cooled."

Dan grinned.

Jim nodded. "Good work, young sleuth," he declared. "Now beat it. Glace an' I are about due to check out."

"Dictate a letter to the Martin baby, an' we'll go look up the numbers in that book you found," he urged when Dan had vanished. "Gimme a buzz when you're ready."

I followed his suggestion, ordered the letter mailed to the sorority house which Miss Martin had given as her address, and put on my hat.

AT THE court house, a clerk was placed at our disposal, and inside a very few minutes we were assured that Richfield's theory concerning the book had been correct.

There followed the slower but necessary work of checking our list and gaining an insight into the nature of the specific cases to which the notations applied.

Here our clerk displayed an interest he made no effort to disguise. But that was not surprising. Margaret Kenton had been a court reporter, and her dramatic death had set official tongues abuzz.

"A shocking thing, Miss Kenton's death," he said.

"Yeah. But what makes you say so?" Bryce inquired.

"Because I can't help wondering if there is any connection between it and the cases she reported, Mr. Bryce," the fellow smiled.

"Meanin' she reported these?" Jim asked.

"All of them, unless I'm mistaken. Most of them were reported in chambers, if you'll notice. She did a lot of that sort of work."

"She was a regular go-getter. Ran a business of her own, and was secretary of the Realty Investment Corporation."

"Yeah?" Save for a narrowing of his lids, Bryce gave no sign that the information concerning Miss Kenton's past activities had aroused his interest.

"Yes," the clerk assented, nodding. "She was a mighty intelligent woman. Her company did a good business, too. One of their stunts was buying up ground that had to be sold in settling up an estate. They did a lot of that till the bottom fell out of real estate. Since then, they haven't done so well. But who has?"

"If you're askin' me, I don't know," Bryce said. "And I never heard of that company in my life. Who was behind it?"

"Why—I don't know." The clerk eyed him. "Their papers are on file, if you'd like to see them."

"Sure," Jim accepted. "Let's give 'em a slant."

"There's just a chance," he said, when the clerk had moved away.

"Of what?" I questioned.

"Another racket," he scowled. "Buyin' up parcels of real estate.

That dame useta know the value of every kind of dirt.—See if this realty corporation wasn't just her an' a bunch of dummy directors."

Seemingly, his guess was right. Because when the articles of incorporation were laid before us they showed the names of one man, and three women besides Miss Kenton, under a date now four years past.

"Four hens an' a rooster," my partner grinned. "Who was the Jonathan Dobbie who was scratchin' with all these clucks?"

The man nodded wisely.

"I wouldn't wonder if he was the guy who put up the money," the clerk replied. "He's a professional bondsman."

"Bondsman!" Bryce exclaimed. "You mean Johnny Dobbie? Well, I'll be a so-and-so! An' he was president of this here realty investment aggregation. I begin to see a light! Yep. She probably got to know him when she was a court reporter. He might be just the lad to make money out of real estate."

"How do you mean—he might be?" the county employee questioned.

I read a puzzled conjecture in his eyes.

BUT BRYCE took a leaf from Dual's book. "I don't know, son. I reckon I was just thinkin' out loud. So—these folks used to handle land that was part of estates?"

"Yes."

The clerk's tone was suddenly guarded. He impressed me as feeling that he had probably said too much.

"And that would mean that land would have to be appraised," Jim considered.

"Yes, but hold on." Our companion's manner was startled. "You don't mean that those appraisements might have been inspired?"

Bryce grinned again. "Inspired is a far-reachin' word. But since you've been inspired to use it, you might follow those transactions through the recorder's office and let us pay you for the work. I'm curious myself. You may find that a lot of the transfers are for 'one dollar and other considerations,' without any indication as to what the other considerations were. Still, hop to it if you care to."

We completed our check on the list, in each case setting the names of the principals against its number. And with the final result in Jim's pocket, we thanked the clerk for his assistance and left.

"Do you really think Dobbie may have arranged for appraisements low enough to guarantee a profit on any reasonable turn over?" I asked, when we again were in my car.

Jim frowned. "The only objection to it is that there's more than one appraiser," he said. "The question is, could he have lined 'em up on that sort of a deal without somebody lettin' out a squawk? Of course we don't know that there really was any crooked work. It's just that I don't expect a Smell of roses when I'm messin' around a skunk. We'd better put Johnson wise to this list, and on what Dan hung on the gig. But let's go to the office first."

AND SO it was that we found the communication devised by pasting together words and letters clipped from the daily papers. The envelope containing it lay upon my desk, flaunting a special delivery stamp and a typed address, but no return destination.

I slit the heavy manilla, and drew from it a sheet of paper folded around five one-hundred-dollar notes!

Holding them somewhat gingerly, I read the message pasted on the inner side of the wrapping paper.

> USE THIS TO HELP O'NEIL. MARGARET KENTON GOT WHAT SHE DESERVED. BUT I DON'T WANT AN INNOCENT MAN TO FRY FOR MY JOB.

Bryce says I gasped. Possibly I did. Because if the thing meant anything at all, those last two words must mean that Margaret Kenton's murderer knew we were working in O'Neil's behalf. It was a taunt, a challenge. It was like a slap in the face.—And five one-hundred-dollar bills!— Hendricks had paid five hundred dollars for silence. But what, then, of Dan's story concerning the purchase of a ring with bills of the proper serial numbers?

"Say, snap out of it, willya? What you got there?"

Jim's voice sounded gruffly in my ears, and I literally thrust the pasted missive into his hands and waited while he read it. And then I spread the currency fanwise before his eyes.

"Five hundred," I said. "In hundred-dollar bills!"

A slow grin tugged at his lips.

"A plant, old son," he decided. "Just a plant. Whoever sent 'em wasn't wise to the fact that we knew that the gig had spent the originals. Where was this thing mailed?"

I glanced at the postmark on the cover. It was that of a small town some thirty miles away, and the mailing date was that of the day before. I told him, and he grinned again.

"Clever—damned clever!" he said. "But just a little too late, unless the Ingham cutie sent it."

"Ingham—?" I began.

The shrill of the telephone cut me off. I grabbed it, answered, stood with the receiver jammed to my ear while a voice barked at me, goaded me afresh with the information it conveyed.

"No, I don't," I said when at length it ceased. "I wrote her this morning. We'll be over as quickly as we can make it."

I slid the receiver back on its cradle. I was baffled and confused.

"That was Johnson," I said, "He's asking about Miss Martin. He's had a call from her sorority house. They say she went out last night and hasn't been heard of since."

Palloni!" Bryce erupted the word, and struck the desk with his fist. "Palloni for a thousand!—Let's get goin'! Here's one time a woman didn't talk too much. Only, that big shot didn't know it when he grabbed her."

CHAPTER X

A SNATCHING

"GET PALLONI," HE urged in the detectives' room at the station. "Get that lousy bum an' sweat him! Slip him the news that for once he's put the finger on himself."

"Yeah," Johnson nodded, scowling. "I reckon he's engineered a snatch. The girl's rich, an' she probably let him know it, the same as she did you—the little cluck. The girl who called me said somebody telephoned the Martin frill, last evenin', an' pretty soon a car drove up an' took her off. One way an' another, Joe's made money out of women."

"The rat!" Bryce growled.

"Sure." Johnson nodded again. "I don't reckon he's got her in any place he owns, though.

"If he really is back of her disappearance, he's probably got her in some other hide out. But I'm havin' him brought in.—Put me wise to what you've done."

We told him, and I gave him the pasted-together letter. He read it and punched a button.

"Have this examined for prints," he directed the orderly who answered, and waited until the man was gone.

"Funny thing about that is—it fits," he said with a humorless grin. "I stuck a tail on the Ingham cutie, and last night she an' Torrance drive over to where this was mailed. They stop at a drug store, an' then come home again. That redhead has been tryin' to sell us the notion that O'Neil is innocent, an' this thing is just about as fancy a bit of work as a woman might cook up. So, outside the money, it's simply, a hunk of mud in your eye."

"I thought of Ingham," Bryce rejoined. "She knows Richfield, an' a clever mouthpiece might shake the thing under the nose of a jury."

He paused at the sound of a rap on the door.

"Come in!" Johnson bawled.

Palloni entered the room, a lowering expression on his features.

"Say," he demanded, helping himself to a chair, "what's the idear of sendin' a prowl car for me. I got a car of my own."

"An' what was it doin' last night?" Johnson rumbled. "Where was it, between say nine o'clock an' whatever time you got home?"

The glances of the two men crossed. Palloni reminded me of a dangerous beast—a product of modern times so crassly careless men of his type were permitted to exist. On the other hand, Johnson gave the impression of a man with his moral feet on a firmer ground.

Palloni shrugged.

"It was waitin' for me outside the Moon. But what the hell!"

"You're dead sure it was waitin', Joe?" Johnson asked.

"Say," the gangster breathed deeply. "What's eatin' you this mornin'? Come on! What's it all about?"

"Okay," Johnson rasped. "I'm asking you if it was waitin', because Allison Martin was snatched last night?"

"An' who in hell is Allison Martin?" Not a muscle twitched in Palloni's face.

BUT JOHNSON merely nodded.

"Pretty good, Joe—but not good enough. You know the kid, all right. She's played around with you a lot.

"This time you picked a hot one, Joe. That cutie's dynamite. An' in snatchin' her last night, you've put the finger on yourself. Ain't *that* a laugh?"

"I don't getcha. I don't getcha at all." Palloni leaned a trifle forward, with slitted lids.

Johnson smiled. "Wise to the Kenton dame's racket, wasn't you, Joe?"

"Wait a minute," Palloni protested. "What's that got to do with this kid's bein' snatched?"

"Why," Johnson said, "Kenton wrote the Martin twist a letter demandin' kale to keep her from tellin' her guardian about her playin' around with you. Quit stallin', Joe. Your back's against the ropes. The Martin girl showed that note to you, and—what you ain't hep to yet—she showed it to Glace and Bryce here, and told 'em what you said about puttin' the heat on Kenton, if she muscled in on your prowl. Then the Kenton twist is gunned, an' last night the Martin kid disappears. Careless work, Joe! You're losing your fine hand!"

Palloni's color faded. His skin was like dirty wax. I saw that he was afraid, like so many of his ilk when faced by danger to themselves. All at once his forehead was beaded by tiny drops of sweat.

Yet he managed another shrug.

"Maybe I ain't the only one who's careless," he snarled. "Or maybe you're tired of your job. Try puttin' the heat on me, if you think it's healthy. There's people will put you back on a beat in the sticks, if I say the word, or if it'd suit you better, they'll kick you off the force. Who in hell are you, to treat me like a bum an' sweat me? I ain't got no reason to be afraid of the police."

"And still, you are, Joe." Johnson's voice was unruffled, cold.

"Says you!" the gangster sneered. "Listen, you cheap cop. The tail don't wag the dog. It's the head does that, an' I own it—I own it! Do you get me?"

"Why, yes, Joe," Johnson nodded. "I happen to know that you and your dirty money are hand in glove with every sort of law enforcement, from cops to courts. If it wasn't for that, you'd have been where you belong before this—you and every yellow dog of a crook that's been playin' hell with the country, the last few years.

"But listen, mug, I may be a cheap cop, but I ain't cheap enough for you or your money to frighten me or buy me. There's still a few people who believe in decency and straight shootin'. I ain't fool enough to expect the tail to wag the dog. But I've heard of the dog's head bein'—cut off."

"Oh, blah!" the gangster challenged. "You can't hang anything on me. I didn't have the Kenton twist knocked off. Try go in' any further with this an'—I'll show you."

"Yeah. An' meanwhile, I'll hold you, Joe," Johnson said.

"Hold me!" Palkmi's jaw sagged. "Say—have you gone clean off your nut? My mouthpiece will spring me so quick it will make you dizzy. You ain't got nothin' to hold me for!"

"EXCEPT MURDER, Joe."

Johnson's voice was actually soft. I admired his self-control. All the mobsman's bluster backed by official crookedness as we knew, had failed to move him. It was Palloni who again reacted to the quietly spoken words.

"Murder?—By God, Johnson, you try to hang that girl's croakin' on me an' I'll—"

"Listen, Joe. You talk too much. Maybe you know it; maybe that's the real reason the Martin kid was snatched. She'd heard you threaten Kenton. But if anything happens to her—if she ain't back here mighty sudden—that murder charge is apt to double up. Think I don't know who's takin' your money, big boy? Well, I do—an' I got a lot of evidence. Right now, I got a coupla witnesses to the fact that you say you own the head of this department.—Hang anything on you, Joe? Why, all I got to do is let you talk, an' hang yourself."

Palloni blinked and shook his head, like a fighter shaken by a staggering punch. "But look," he said, in almost whining fashion. "There ain't no sense in this. Let's you an' me get together. I don't know a thing about this snatchin', but if it would help, I might find out. If this Martin frail was to show up—"

"*If,*" Johnson cut in sharply. "You mean *when,* don't you, Joe? If I hold you until she does—"

"You damned fool!" Palloni's tone was hoarse. "I told you I'd walk out on a writ, if you tried it."

"Yeah. I heard you," Johnson agreed. "But thanks for the tip. When you do. I'll arrest you for murder. An' if they spring you on that, I'll think of a lot of things you've pulled in the past. Looks like your mouthpiece might have to earn his money for a day or two, Joe. Let's get goin'. You're under arrest. Now—" He reached for the telephone. "Do you want to call your lawyer?"

"Yeah." Palloni moved to the desk.

"Outside call," Johnson spoke to the switch, and extended the receiver.

Palloni caught it from him and called a number.

"This is Joe Palloni. I gotta talk to Richfield. It's important."

Johnson's expression was blank. I met Jim's eyes, and no doubt he grinned at what he read in my face. Because here was Palloni, overlord of the underworld, speaking to Richfield with a commanding tongue.

Then he was thrusting the receiver into Johnson's hand, growling:

"Here—he'll talk to you himself."

JOHNSON WAS adjusting the instrument to his ear.

"Hello, Richfield," he said. "Joe's just tipped us off that he owned the Department, from the commissioner down. An' seein' that he did it before a coupla friends of mine, I slapped him under arrest. How long till I can look for a writ to spring him?— What?—Oh, about the girl he just mentioned? Nope. That ain't quite all of it. There's a little matter of murder—a hook-up with the Kenton case.—Sure, I could do that if you say so.—Okay, I'll send him over."

His glance lifted to Palloni. "All right, Joe. He wants to see you. Scram out of here," he advised.

"An' that's how we call your bluff!" the gangster rasped.

"Well, maybe." Johnson replaced the receiver on its rest. "But I wouldn't be too sure of it. There's a thing called history, Joe, an' the darned thing's got a habit of repeatin'. It's funny about these United States. The people will stand for a lot and then some day—*blooie!* They grab an ax an' chop off the dog's head. Tell Richfield I'm givin' you twenty-four hours to get that girl back to school."

For a moment, Palloni made no move. Then he rested a hand on the desk.

"I'll get you for this, Johnson," he rasped. "I'll get you. It's a promise!"

"I don't doubt it, Joe," Johnson said, and looked him in the eyes. "I ain't sure a bunch of your gorillas didn't try it out on the West Park viaduct, when they sideswiped my machine last night. Still, it's mighty careless of you to say anything like that before other folks. As I told you, you talk too much.—Now, you scram over an' see Richfield, an' tell him I'm givin' you twenty-four hours—from right now."

"Arrh!" Palloni voiced an animal snarl, spun on his feet, and went out.

"Did you mean that?" Bryce demanded. "About what happened to us last night?"

"I don't know, of course," Johnson scowled. "But I wouldn't be surprised. There's one thing certain—whoever is back of the Kenton killin' is havin' us tailed as close as we'd tail him, if we knew who he was. As for the Martin girl, I'm lookin' for results. Richfield's clever. That's why Palloni pays his price.— Now, about this realty investment stuff. It's apt to be crooked, if Dobbie's in it. You seein' Dual to-night?"

"Sure." Jim nodded.

"Okay," Johnson said. "I'm after the dope on the gig. If I get it, I'll go with you.—Just a minute!" He lifted the telephone and spoke to the Identification Bureau, grunted acceptance.

"The only prints on your letter was yours an' mine.—Let's eat. It's after one."

WE LUNCHED, then went back and saw O'Neil, to little result. The man was sunk in a depth of brooding, from which he was difficult to rouse.

He admitted that Miss Kenton had known Cerra. "I never liked the fellow, myself," he said.

"Did he speak to her, or come to your table, the other night?" I asked.

"Why—" O'Neil began, and frowned. "He didn't come to the table; but he—he sort of twiddled his thumb and finger at her from a distance—just before she sent me to the check room— My God, Mr. Glace, do you think it could have been a signal, and that she sent me away so she could speak with him? Do you think he—?"

"We don't yet know what we think," said Jim. "Did you see him afterward, O'Neil?"

"No." O'Neil shook his head. "Say, stop it, will you? Stop making me think such things."

"Okay, son," Bryce assented. "What brand of cigarettes did Miss Kenton smoke?"

"Why, the same as I do." O'Neil scowled and drew a pack from his pocket. "What's that got to do with the thing? The whole thing's crazy. Richfield asked me about it this morning. Only he wanted to know about Dick and Gladys, too. He said it might be a means of proving my innocence. But's that insane."

"Maybe not," said Jim. "Did either Torrance or Miss Ingham smoke a Turkish cigarette?"

"Turkish? You mean scented?" O'Neil said vaguely. "Why, no.—But that damned gigolo did! I know, because I hate the odor; and once, when he did come to our table, he lit one, smoked part of it, and ground out the butt before he left."

"Ground it out, huh?"

"Yes—rubbed the end of it in an ash tray, you know," O'Neil nodded.

Bryce interrupted. "Did Miss Kenton ever tell you that she was the secretary of a real estate corporation?"

"Why, yes. The Realty Investment Corporation," O'Neil assented at once. "They bought up mortgages, the way I understood it, and sold the property at a profit. Margaret had a brilliant business sense, you know."

"She sure did," Bryce agreed, and once more changed the subject. "Seen Miss Ingham to-day?"

"No. But I'm expecting her this afternoon," O'Neil replied. "I told her not to come, but she insisted that she would. She's— like that."

"Most women are," Jim said dryly. "An' if she runs true to form, you tell her we'd like to see her."

When we had left the cell, Jim said, I got more than a hunch that that dancin' man was in the Kenton frail's room *after* she was gunned.

"What's the idea of leaving word for Miss Ingham to call?" I asked.

Bryce chuckled. "I was thinkin' we might ask her if she mailed that five hundred to us, last night."

"And you think she'd tell you?"

"Well, that's an open question," he grinned. "But she might, without meanin' to, if I asked her sudden. Anyway, I'd like to hear what she says about bein' over there with Torrance last night."

CHAPTER XI

THREAT OF THE MOON

MISS INGHAM'S EXPLANATION was simple when she faced us in the office that afternoon. Torrance had found that he must make a business trip to the neighboring hamlet, and he had asked her to drive along.

"But how did you know?" she questioned.

"Is your friend Johnson having us—shadowed, as I think they call it?" she added.

"Johnson's doin' what any good cop ought to," Jim returned.

"And"—a faint smile twisted Miss Ingham's lips—"beyond the fact that I went riding, has he discovered anything?"

"Nothing definite," I told her. "But we've picked up a few things."

"Such as the sort of cigarette Johnny Cerra smokes," she suggested. "Bob told me about that line of investigation. Where did you find it?"

"In an ash tray," Jim said. "In an ash tray in Marge Kenton's rooms."

"I see." Miss Ingham knit her brows. "But would that really make it appear that he might have killed her?"

"If it did, he'd be where your boy friend is now," Jim said in a grumpy tone.

"Bob's dreadfully worked up about it," Miss Ingham declared. "He still doesn't know what Marge was doing, of course. But it seems to me he's beginning to suspect that there was another side to her life. It's rather dreadful to watch—the death of faith.

I don't know what he'll do when he knows.—Her death was like her life, wasn't it, Mr. Glace? I mean there was something sinister; something deep and hidden about it?"

"There was plenty hidden," Jim made his attack. "Part of it bein' the identity of the person who sent us five hundred dollars to use in O'Neil's behalf, from that town where you went with Torrance, last night."

The girl took it between the eyes and did not flinch. "And you were thinking I might have mailed it, were you? Did you think I'd tell you, if I had?"

"Well, I wanted to see how you'd act when we threw it at you," Jim replied. "How old are you, Miss Ingham?"

"Old enough to know better than that, Mr. Bryce." Miss Ingham smiled. "But to answer your question, I was twenty-four on the sixteenth of last month. Does Johnson think I may have mailed the money? If he does, I won't hold it against him. I'm beginning to realize that he can't play favorites. But to have done such a thing after I had asked you to work for Bob strikes me as ridiculous. Does Mr. Richfield know about it?"

"Not yet," I said.

Save for her question I would have believed her wholly ignorant of the matter.

But in it she had touched at last on the most probable purpose behind the mailing of that curious, pasted-together communication—its effect on a jury in O'Neil's behalf.

Her next words only made matters worse.

"Don't you think he should be told?" she asked.

"Oh, I reckon he will be," Bryce said, gruffly.

The woman laughed in brittle fashion.

"Meaning I'll tell him? You don't trust me, do you, Mr. Bryce? Maybe that's my fault, in saying I'd do anything to help Bob. But I meant that. I'll do anything to keep him from suffering more than he already has, through Marge."

"An' I'm dead sure of that," Jim told her.

"Guard the man Cerra closely," Semi-Dual warned.

"I see." She crinkled her lids. "You're as blunt as a policeman, Mr. Bryce."

"Well, I was one once." Jim grinned. "But—we're backin' O'Neil ourselves."

"I know." Miss Ingham's expression softened. "And I think I'd better be going, unless there's something else."

"Nope." Jim shook his head.

"Then good afternoon—and good luck." The girl smiled again in a wistful fashion as she rose.

"SURPRISIN' HER is like tryin' to make a cat fall any way but on its feet," Jim grumbled when she was gone. "An' she saw right away how Richfield could use that letter with a jury. Now, if Johnson gets the dope Dual wants on Cerra."

Johnson did; and once he was in the inner room of the tower, he laid the written information, together with the communication we had received, on Semi's desk.

Dual glanced at the latter. "No marks of identification?" he inquired.

"Nope." Johnson shook his head.

"The probable work of the murderer," Dual began his

comment. "It is perhaps a gesture in self defense. And as such, it is quite in keeping with the atmosphere of secrecy and sinister scheming which has marked our problem from the first. Inasmuch as both individuals were seemingly actuated by wholly selfish motives, I cannot read into the transmittal of the money or the communication anything more than a deceptive effort, inspired by and in harmony with the character complex to which the sender is polarized.—Your patience for a time, now, if you please."

He turned to the desk and plunged into a series of calculations, while the three of us sat and watched.

A great clock ticked in a corner. Bryce smoked one of his deadly appearing cigars. Johnson sat frowning as though the spell of the moment weighed upon him. It was eerie, uncanny to watch the man at the desk, as he read once more a riddle of the stars.

Then he was speaking. "Gladys Ingham is Venus. We contact once more the element of love—but a love more natural and normal, as opposed to the degraded love of Neptune. Furthermore, a love which I feel will exert itself unreservedly in O'Neil's behalf. As for Miss Martin, I see her as the Moon; but in the major instance her influence is not important save as a danger to yourselves."

"Danger?" Johnson echoed gruffly. "Through Palloni?"

"Let us consider that question in its order," Dual said after a pause. "Miss Kenton's connection with the Realty Investment Corporation is of interest. Saturn, which exercised an evil influence in her destiny, may quite consistently have inspired her dealings in real estate. Saturn is of the earth, and when evilly posited, may excite suspicion as to the legality of her operations. The man Dobbie is seemingly not above reproach."

"He's so crooked he'd cheat at solitaire!" said Bryce.

"That being the case," Dual went on, "I would advise that you examine the Recorder's books yourselves."

"Okay," Jim agreed. "We'll send Dan down in the mornin'.—

Now, do you reckon my findin' that cigarette stub might mean that the gig cleaned out that drawer in her rooms?"

"Perchance he carried away a message from the gods," said Semi-Dual. "I regard him of importance, because of his similar influence in the lives of both Neptune and Mars."

"**AND TO** what star do you hitch Palloni?" Johnson inquired.

"Saturn, inspector," Dual replied. "Permit me to compliment you on your attitude toward him this morning. It would appear to have embodied firmness with a well considered finesse. But do you consider it well to have let him know that you were in possession of evidence against any one high in the forces of law and order?"

"Why—" Johnson actually blushed before that blending of praise and caution, "I don't know as it was. But you see, what he said was true enough to hurt. An' I ain't afraid of that gorilla."

"Afraid, no." Dual smiled slightly. "But a cornered beast will fight. As you are aware, ever since I have known you I have kept the horoscopes of yourself and my friends Glace and Bryce. You escaped by a narrow margin last night, but you escaped. Which brings me to your question of a few moments ago. I find indications in all three charts of a further danger of which I feel it my duty to warn you."

"Through the Martin skirt?" Jim demanded.

"Through the Moon, and Saturn," Dual returned. "Palloni sees in you now a future as well as a present threat to the immunity he has so long enjoyed. He also sees a danger through Inspector Johnson to those from whom that immunity has been obtained. Should he accede to Johnson's demands, he might temporarily abate the situation, but with a loss of prestige. Still, if he could possibly destroy you, he might remove your menace to his future operations, and reestablish the security of all involved."

"Yeah," Jim nodded in comprehension. "An' there's a way he could do it, easy. If instead of bringin' or sendin' that girl back, he was to—"

THE SHRILL of a telephone cut off his words. It tensed my every nerve, because Dual's number was not listed. It was known to only a few, among whom were Johnson and Bryce and myself.

I waited as Semi-Dual drew the instrument from a compartment in his desk and answered.

"He is here," he said, and held the instrument toward Johnson. "For you, inspector."

Johnson seized it, barked a response, waited while a distant voice snapped and crackled in the receiver.

"Okay," he said in decision at length. "Have a squad car ready when I get there."

"That was the station," he announced, and set the instrument on the desk. "I left your number with 'em, Mr. Dual. An' they just got a rumble on that Martin skirt. A call just come in from a pay station, to the effect that we could find her in an old house about five miles beyond the end of Park Drive Boulevard."

"And you intend going there, inspector?" Dual inquired.

"Why—sure," Johnson said, and paused. "I reckon you think we're up against the danger we were discussin'. But that's in my line of duty."

"Precisely," said Semi-Dual, and I saw his gray eyes light in appreciation of Johnson's attitude. "And a man's duty is a thing he may not shirk. However, forewarned is forearmed. The nature of your venture coincides with indications which I have found in your several astral charts. Therefore, do not walk blindly into some trap, in which this girl is made the bait. Besides the squad car you have already ordered, let me advise that you have a second car follow you, inspector, and that it carry armed and dependable men, known to yourself."

"That's good advice," Johnson declared. "I'll take it. Now, is there anything else?"

"Nothing essential," said Semi-Dual. "Until you return, I shall devote myself to the astral findings, as applying to the man Giovanni Cerra."

"Okay," Johnson nodded. "Come along, boys! Let's give that gorilla a surprise."

CHAPTER XII

TRAP BAIT

AT THE STATION a squad car awaited. Johnson saw to the second car himself. To it he assigned four men, among them one by the name of Mulcahy, who had seen service in a machine gun company overseas.

The inspector gave his directions briefly.

"I know where this hideout is. There's a gas station four miles out, an' then a lane on the left, about one mile farther. The house is a half mile up it, back of a stand of trees. Give us three minutes an' then follow.—Okay. We're off."

We piled into the squad car and roared away into the night, Johnson with a machine rifle between his knees.

Bryce cleared his throat. "What I can't see is how Joe could think we'd fall for it," he grumbled.

"We are fallin' for it, ain't we?" Johnson rasped. "If it hadn't been for Dual—"

"Yeah," Jim chuckled. "He grabs a pencil, says we're runnin' into danger, an' then says he'll devote himself to the Jumpin' Jack's horrible horoscope till we get back. Comfortin' thought!"

"As indicating that we *will* get back?" I suggested.

"Sure," said Jim. "I'd hate not to. I'm anxious to see how this Kenton deal turns out. Joe's probably at the Moon, right now."

"Yeah. And he'll have a steel-ribbed alibi," Johnson growled.

We sped swiftly along the Park Drive Boulevard, with its flare of a multitude of lights and traffic. By swift degrees the cars dwindled in numbers as we reached the open country and raced along a night-shrouded road.

At last Johnson spoke to the chauffeur:

"Slow down, Andy. We turn left a mile from that last filling station."

"Then this must be the place."

The chauffeur brought the car to a stand opposite a narrow lane that angled off from the highway.

"You wanta go in there?"

"Yeah," Johnson assented. "An' we're apt to run into trouble.— Keep your eyes peeled."

"Okay."

The driver meshed his gears. The car bumped into the narrow track, crowned between bordering ditches, as I saw in the glow of the head lights, beyond which the shadowy bulk of bushes and trees pressed close.

"Lovely place for a murder!" the driver grumbled. "Just what, if anything, are we expectin'?"

" 'Anything' about sums it up," said Johnson. "It's a cinch they know we're comin' an'— Hey! Look out!"

Beyond us the head lights picked up the shape of a dark car. But even as Johnson voiced his warning, I saw a flicker of flame stab from it in interrupted flashes, heard the coughing chatter of a machine gun, the patter of bullets striking metal, the tinkle of splintering glass. And I heard the driver groan as he sagged at the wheel and our car shot drunkenly into the ditch.

"Keep down!" I heard Johnson's voice again. He kicked the door open and slid through it with the machine gun in his grasp.

Bryce and I followed as best we could.

Once more, the machine flared from the car beyond us. Its missiles rattled above us as we crouched. Then, as it ceased, we managed to drag the driver's body out of the car and into the ditch.

He still breathed and moaned as we laid him down in a smother of dead weeds.

"Now—if they'll only do that once more," Johnson grated with a deadly note in his words.

And as though the words were a cue, again the machine gun rattled.

Johnson's rifle answered, from where he had crept a little farther along the ditch, to fire at the other weapon's flash.

I THOUGHT I heard a scream from a stricken throat, then the fire from the dark car ceased.

"Got him! Got him!" Johnson croaked. "Now if Mulcahy has done what I told him."

The roar of a speeding motor came to my ears. It came toward us, nearer and nearer. I turned my head back along the road. Twin lights were rushing toward us, swinging and rolling to the unevenness of the track.

They came nearer, nearer—slowed—came to a standstill.

"Inspector!" a brusk voice challenged.

"Okay, Mulcahy," Johnson called direction. "Burn down that car up the road."

"And how!"

The police weapon went into action. For possibly twenty seconds it sprayed lead on the car beyond us.

"And there you are, inspector," Mulcahy shouted. "Anything in it is mincemeat."

"Bring your gang up here," Johnson said as he crawled out of the ditch, and in a moment the others joined us. "Come along," he said, and led the way to the other machine.

Bryce and I followed, to stand with the rest about a figure huddled on the ground.

"Make him?" Johnson questioned, as Mulcahy turned the body over.

"Yeah." Mulcahy nodded. "One of Palloni's baboons. An'—there's an other."

He directed the ray of a flash light upon the rear seat of a car, where a dead man's face, torn by gunfire, was revealed by its searching beam. "Well, where do we go from here?"

"Up the road. We gotta go through a house," Johnson told him. "Leave two of your men to look after Andy. They got him, first crack."

"An' paid for it. Good work, inspector," Mulcahy grated. "We heard the guns.—Where is he?"

We examined the driver and found his wounds to be less serious than we feared. Then we piled into the other machine and drove on up the road.

TWO MINUTES brought us to an unlighted house. Nor was there any sign of life about it, as we advanced with our weapons ready. We mounted a porch, but there was no answer as Johnson hammered on the door with a police weapon.

He kicked the door open and led the way into a hallway. There, by the ray of his torch, we found an uncarpeted stair.

"Stay here," he addressed Mulcahy. "Get anything that stirs.—The rest of you come up."

We mounted the stairs and at the top we paused.

"Miss Martin!" Johnson called.

"Yes—yes. I'm—in here," a feminine voice replied.

Johnson chuckled softly. "Plain enough," he growled. "They figured they'd get us, an' come back for her. Well, right now they're both in hell, I reckon."

He walked to a door and flung it open to show Allison Martin, clad in a pink corduroy robe, standing wide-eyed in the center of a room illuminated by the flicker of a candle.

"Well, well! What are you doing here?" he smiled.

"They—kidnaped me," Miss Martin faltered, and caught sight of Jim and me. "Oh, Mr. Glace—Mr. Bryce!"

"Present," Jim answered, grinning. "How do you like gangsters for playmates now, Miss Martin?"

"Oh—please!" Miss Martin begged. "Please don't. I was—so

frightened when I heard that shooting! And that old woman took away my clothes. Won't you try to find them and get me away from here?"

"Well, pink's becomin' to a blonde," said Jim.

We found her clothing in a closet, but of the old woman she had mentioned there was no trace. In five minutes she was dressed. We got her into the car, drove back, and dragged our own machine out of the ditch. Then, with the wounded chauffeur and the bodies of the dead gangsters, we drove back to town.

At the station Allison Martin told her story.

"I never dreamed of such a thing. I got a telephone call and somebody said he was Billy Gregg. Billy's the brother of a girl who graduated last spring, and I don't know him awfully well. But he said he was in town and would I go some place and dance.

"Well, we'd done that before, a few times, and so I said all right. When a car drove up I ran out, and somebody grabbed me and dragged me in and held his hand over my mouth so I couldn't scream. I tried to fight, and he choked me and told me to 'cut it out!' Then, when I was nearly strangled, he said, 'If I ease up on your pipe will you be good?' I nodded, and he tied a cloth over my eyes. Then we got to a house, and they took me upstairs. An old woman took away my clothes and gave me that corduroy robe and a pair of felt slippers."

SHE LAUGHED, but I caught a touch of hysteria in the sound.

"I don't believe I'll ever care for corduroy again! But I was glad of it, last night. I never went in for this nudist stuff. So I put the robe on, and the old woman gave me some cigarettes, a glass of milk and some magazines. Then she went out and locked the door.—I thought of everything.

"The door was locked; the windows were nailed down; and I knew if I broke the glass somebody in the house would probably hear it. I thought of setting fire to the house, but after I realized I'd have to start the blaze in that room, with me in nothing but a pink kimona, the idea didn't seem so hot. Anyway, after

I'd thought it over I wasn't so badly scared. You see, I've been a good deal of a fool of late."

"I know you have," Johnson told her, grinning.

"Well, let it go, then." She flushed. "The more I thought about it, the surer I felt that my being kidnaped was just a play to get some money; and I felt sure I knew the party who had framed the whole thing up. Because he knew I had money of my own, and he also knew about Billy Gregg. That is, he'd seen me with Billy, and had asked me about him, once when he was in town before. And about their using his name—"

"You used your head," said Johnson admiringly.

"Sure. After not using it had run me into a pink kimona and a pair of bedroom slippers."

Miss Martin giggled.

"So I smoked and read a while and then I went to bed. In the morning I tried to see what I could from a window, but it wasn't much. The old woman brought me some breakfast, but nobody else came near me. I wondered why they didn't, and why they didn't ask me to write for money. Then I remembered a note I'd got a few days ago—"

"The one you showed Joe Palloni?" Johnson asked.

"Uh-huh." Miss Martin nodded. "He said something about the writer muscling in on his prowl, when I showed it to him; and then I began to see where I'd been his prowl, all right. Of course, after what I'd told him about myself he wouldn't need to write anything, because he knew enough to handle the whole transaction himself. Oh, sure—I figured it all out.

"Then, earlier this evening, I heard voices downstairs. And after a long time, what sounded like shooting. All at once I was scared cold, and I sat there praying. Then you called.—I'm terribly sorry. Was your driver badly hurt?"

"He'll get over it," Johnson assured her. "You couldn't identify the men who grabbed you, could you?"

"No-o." Miss Martin shook her head. "Ever try riding blindfolded? It was like a nightmare, sort of. There wasn't a thing but the sound of the engine, and now and then a bump. Maybe I deserved it. But I think the note I showed Palloni was enough."

"Don't worry about that," Jim said, and explained his meaning.

"Then he—knew her?" Miss Martin cried. "Do you think he had her killed? Oh, dear! I feel as though I was responsible for things I never dreamed of; for her being shot, and your driver being wounded, and those two men being killed to-night. I—I've been worse than silly."

She lifted a hand and crushed the knuckles against her lips.

"Here, here! I'm going to send you home now." He lifted a telephone and ordered a car. "Come on now," he said and rose to lead her out.

QUITE UNEXPECTEDLY, he was accompanied by another and wholly strange young woman, when he returned.

"Gettin' to be a ladies' man," he declared as he flopped back into his chair. "Miss Evelyn Gore, here, runs an elevator in the Willden. Sit down, Miss Gore, and tell us what it's all about."

"Why—" the girl said as she took a chair. "Remember the other night, how you got me out of bed and asked me if I'd seen anybody go up to Miss Kenton's room, late the night she was shot? Well, I've remembered. There was a man. Ordinarily she didn't have many callers. There was just Mr. O'Neil, who came a lot; and Mr. Richfield, the lawyer, once or twice; and this other man.

"But the last time he was there was the night before she was killed.—You know, Mr. Richfield's taken charge of her rooms, and he was talking to me to-night, and all at once I remembered. The man who had called on her was slender and dark, and light on his feet—like a dancer, I mean. He always called the number of her apartment, instead of her floor. That's how I knew he was calling on her. So I told the manager I knew something I thought I oughta tell you, and he let me off."

"The gig, by granny!" Bryce declared as Miss Gore paused.

"Gig?" She turned to face him. "Does that mean you know him?—Was he a gigolo really?"

Jim grinned. "The answer to both your questions is—yes."

"Just a gigolo," Miss Gore nodded. "Well, that would explain the way he walked. There ain't much I miss. But I gotta be gettin' back.—I hope they prove Mr. O'Neil ain't guilty. He's—nice."

"And that ties it," Bryce proclaimed, when she had left. "The Jack was there the night before, as well as on the night they rubbed her out. An' the last time, he left his cigarette."

"Yeah," Johnson nodded. "Funny, how things turn out! Danged if Dual ain't right. It's the little things that count, an' keep buildin' up. The way they're stackin' up now, it looks like your snipe hunt might amount to somethin' yet."

CHAPTER XIII

THE BEGINNING OF THE END

"BUILDIN' UP!" JIM said as we walked to where my car was parked. "The Addin' Machine of the Cosmos don't make mistakes. The Wheel goes round and—*click!* There's another item on what Semi calls the Ledger of Life. Buildin' up to what? A sort of balance in which nothin' is wrote off or missed. Makes you wonder, don't it?—Look. We didn't know the gig was in the habit of goin' to the Willden, an' then an elevator girl remembers the way he walks." He chuckled. "Darned if the Addin' Machine don't even take account of a man's gait. You gotta watch your step!"

"In more ways than one," I agreed. "I imagine that Palloni is not as well pleased with the outcome of his plan as we are to-night."

"You win," said Bryce. "To-morrow I'm sendin' Dan to the Recorder's office an' see can he get us a few more straws."

Thanks to that expressed intention, we took the next step in untangling the twisted threads of Margaret Kenton's life—those dark and criminal threads in which, in the end, she became entangled, and which finally brought about her death.

Dan received his instructions and left, and Allison Martin was announced. She came to get her note, and was in a chastened mood.

"If you'll let me have your bill. I'd like to pay it," she said, "though I know that there are things one never can pay for—

things such as you did for me last night; the sort of things you can only give thanks for on your knees."

"Not a bad kid," Bryce said when she had disappeared.

Noon came, and three o'clock, before Dan showed up.

"If there's anything funny about those land deals, I don't know what it is," he began his report. "But I don't know much about the sort of dirt you measure in feet an' rods. Nearly every one of the things was plastered with mortgages. I made a list, if you want to see it.—Here."

He handed some papers to Bryce before he went on:

"There was one thing, though, that I'll bet you wasn't expectin'. That Ingham dame musta worked in some office before she hooked up with the Kenton doll, because you know mortgages have to be sworn to, an' darned if her name wasn't on a lot of these!"

"As a notary?" Bryce said, sharply.

"Yeah." Danny grinned. "Some of 'em was signed by a fellow the clerk said worked for Dobbie till he took pneumonia an' died. But findin' her moniker on 'em made me wonder.— And here's another thing. The Kenton dame hadn't run her steno service more'n two years; so if she was secretary of the Realty Corporation she musta been workin' for Richfield at the time."

Jim reacted to the information with a grunt. A baffled expression came into his eyes.

"Maybe we oughta see Richfield again. How about it, old son?" he said.

I AGREED, and rang the lawyer's office. I met a more cordial welcome than before.

"Come over, of course," he assented. "And by the way, O'Neil says Cerra smokes the brand of cigarette Bryce found in the ash tray, and that Miss Ingham likes 'em toasted."

"You gentlemen seem to be picking up all the threads," he said when we had told him what Dan had learned. "And I can readily see how your question applies. Miss Kenton acted as secretary of the Realty Investment Corporation, with my full knowledge and consent. Dobbie organized it, and I helped with the legal end. As a bondsman, he came in contact with a great many attractive pieces of real estate posted against his bonds. And he evolved the idea of turning his knowledge to a profit. He'd bid in parcels of ground and sell them, and I think he did fairly well for a time. You will recall that I told you that Miss Kenton made money through investments."

"Yes," said Bryce. "But you didn't say what kind."

"I referred to the company we are discussing, none the less," the lawyer explained. "I've handled a good deal of business for Dobbie. He had met Miss Kenton in his office, and he offered her the chance to come into it if she desired. I advised her to accept. I do a pretty good business in the settling of estates, and it frequently happens that bits of land are involved.

"Now and then circumstances make it advisable to convert such holdings into money at a justifiable price. And as I was handling Dobbie's other business, it was natural that I should submit such propositions to him when I deemed it best. A good proportion of such lands were mortgaged, and Dobbie's chance of profits hinged on his ability to buy them at prices low enough to insure them after the mortgage was written off."

"Then the company was really Dobbie?" I said as the attorney paused.

"The stock was largely in his name," he said. "Margaret, however, held a considerable block."

"Miss Ingham ever work for you?" Bryce asked.

"No." Richfield smiled. "She worked for Dobbie. His office is in this building.—Just what is your interest?"

Jim outlined the matter of the notarial signatures, and Richfield frowned.

"Would that mean that you hoped to find something questionable in the transaction, gentlemen?"

I laughed. "Hoped would just about fit, I'm afraid. Actually, we're getting nowhere in our investigations. We haven't so much as a tenable motive, unless Miss Kenton was killed by some one whom she had victimized or was attempting to victimize. Yet the murderer seems to know that we're working for O'Neil.—Has Miss Ingham communicated with you today?"

"No, Mr. Glace," he denied, and I told him of the oddly constructed note we had received.

"Five hundred dollars," he said, and frowned. "There's a macabre quality about the whole thing, Mr. Glace. It's a thing of shadows—a dance of black and white marionettes, rather than a drama of the flesh."

"Precisely," I agreed.

"But there's just a chance I could use that letter in O'Neil's favor," he went on. "I might even be able to free him with it. I've won a case or two on as narrow a margin in the past."

Jim surprised me. "About as narrow as the one that kept Palloni's gorillas from makin' collanders of us last night?" he countered.

SUDDENLY RICHFIELD laughed in a manifest enjoyment of his thrust.

"Haw, haw, haw!—My congratulations on your escape. Needless to say, however, Joe did not follow my advice."

"That bein'?" Jim suggested gruffly.

"That he accede to Johnson's demands." Richfield sobered. "I would be sorry to feel that you thought it might have been anything else. Still—all's well that ends well."

"Yeah." Bryce scowled. "Any chance that Joe or that heat man of his, Tovallo, pulled the Kenton job?"

"No." Richfield's tone was sharp. "He could have carried out his designs with Miss Martin without anything like that."

"Unless he was paid for it," said Bryce.

"And furnished with her gun?" The lawyer smiled.

"Well—" Jim said. "There's always the Jumpin' Jack. He was in her rooms the night before she was knocked off. He could 'a' slipped her gat to Tovallo. That would be in keepin' with that word you just used. *Mac—*"

"*Macabre?*" Richfield smiled. "But I doubt if Cerra stole her gun."

"The point is," said Jim, "that whoever did it was countin' on the unexpected element in the job to keep him safe."

"Right." Richfield nodded. "But your clever criminal refrains from—shall we say—lost motion, Mr. Bryce. He makes the fewest possible moves. Personally, I feel that if Margaret's gun was actually stolen, the one who took it hoped that her death might be counted suicide. Now, however, the murderer's best strategy is to remain inactive and let O'Neil bear the brunt of suspicion until—as I sincerely hope—we have established his innocence."

"So he sends us five yards an' a crazy note," Jim made comment. "You find anything in her papers that might help?"

"No," Richfield said. "I've seen the will, and some private papers. If there really were any such records as you suggest, I'm afraid they were in some place which I have not discovered—or were actually removed. You're having Cerra watched?"

"Naturally." Jim rose. "Thanks for the time we've wasted."

As we left, Jim asked the elevator operator for Dobbie's office.

"What's the notion?" I asked as we moved down a corridor to where the bondsman's name was lettered on frosted glass.

"Keep your ears pinned back," he growled, and led the way into the office. There was a straining purposefulness in his face.

BUT IT was gone when we faced Jonathan Dobbie, across the desk at which he sat.

"Only want a minute of your time, Mr. Dobbie," he said. "We know Margaret Kenton was secretary of the Realty Investment Corporation, of which you are president."

"What about it?"

Dobbie glanced at the card a stenographer had taken to him

before we were sent in. He was a man with a pasty complexion, heavy set, with small dark eyes sunk in fatty lids.

"Why, I reckon her bein' killed was sort of—unhandy, wasn't it?" Jim said.

I began to see his drift. And so, apparently, did Dobbie. The latter eyed him for an appreciable time before he answered:

"Naturally. But it can't be helped."

"The idea is, that we was wonderin' if, as secretary, she kept the company books in your office or hers?" Bryce pointed out. "We'd like a chance to see 'em, if we could."

Dobbie's flabby body tensed. His dark eyes shifted.

"You're from the police?" he asked.

"Nope," Jim returned. "It's all on our card. But we're workin' for the lad who was pinched for her shootin'."

Dobbie appeared to be relieved, in so far as I could judge.

"Then—you're exceeding your authority, I'm afraid," he decided gruffly.

"Yeah." My partner nodded. "I was afraid you might see it that way. But the trouble is that some of Miss Kenton's records seem to have—er—disappeared. We was wonderin' if your books might be among 'em."

Dobbie's voice took on a rasp. "I don't know what's behind all this, but if you know one-tenth of what you ought to, you know damned well they were not. Those books are in my safe. And if you want to see 'em—"

"Oh, well," Jim interrupted, "if that's so, I reckon we don't. But you see, she was workin' a blackmailin' racket."

"Blackmail!" For an instant Dobbie's face was a sickly mask. "Say, what the hell do you mean by that?"

"Why, nothin'." Jim's voice was soft. "Nothin' at all, if your books are safe. Sorry to have troubled you. S'long, Dobbie"

"And they ain't," he declared the instant we were out of the office. "They ain't safe, old son. That bird's worried right now.

That's why I wanted to see him. There's something phony about those land deals, and he's—worried."

I nodded. I understood. And that night, as we sat with Semi-Dual in his quarters, one of the things I told our host was that Jonathan Dobbie was afraid.

That night marked the real beginning of the end.

CHAPTER XIV

THE BALANCE MOUNTS

DUAL HAD BEGUN to add together the sum of cause and effect on the Ledger of Life, toward that final tragic balance by which the account of the debtor was closed.

Knowledge sat like a mantle upon him, hovering about him like an aura, in the room where the four of us sat. For Johnson was with us, admittedly baffled in the matter of the woman's death.

Dual had heard what we had to tell, when Johnson cleared his throat.

"Yes, inspector?" Dual's gray eyes turned to him.

Johnson grinned in his self-conscious way.

"I was just wondering if we ought to shake down that gig. He's been tailed, and it's got us nothing. But I can't help feelin' that he knows a lot we might use."

"Knowledge," said Semi-Dual, "is a two-edged sword.—I have set up the astral chart of Giovanni Cerra. Saturn threatens him, and Mars."

"By Saturn," Bryce exclaimed, "you mean Palloni?"

"Saturn, who is Palloni, in my estimation," Dual assented. "Hence, guard the man Cerra closely, until you have the knowledge you seek. When speaking with the man Dobbie, did you happen to mention Miss Ingham?"

"No." Jim frowned. "I never thought about her."

Dual put out a hand. "And may I see the list Quinn left with you this afternoon, concerning those real estate transactions?"

I handed it to him, and he ran through it while we waited. Once or twice I saw a furrow of consideration between his eyes. Then once more he was speaking.

"**THERE IS** a possibility here. Danny's record is most complete. It therefore becomes apparent that in a rather large proportion of the real estate firm's transactions the mortgage affecting a specific parcel of land was recorded at a date considerably later than that of the actual document. This may or may not have been of deliberate intent; but if so, might excite a suspicion as to the validity of the whole transaction. What I say must apply as a purely theoretical explanation. But let us assume that the Realty Investment Corporation's operations were not wholly legitimate. They bought lands under mortgage and sold them at a profit. That is, we are led to assume that a profit accrued. But if beyond a normal expectancy the face of the mortgage could be included in that profit—"

"Face of the mortgage?" Bryce broke in sharply. "You mean they might have been—forged?"

Silence followed his words. Their suggestion gripped us with its hint of covert double dealing.

Dual replied: "Strange things happen, during illnesses, or when a man lies dying—or even afterwards. That dead men tell no tales is a fallacy, my friends. At times they speak as surely as though alive. This company frequently dealt in lands that were parts of estates, lands originally owned by persons deceased, save through documents signed or apparently signed before their lips were sealed.

"From the dates of execution and recording in the list I hold, I am led to believe that many of the mortgages in question were only recorded *after* the hand which presumably signed them was cold."

"Holy cat!" Jim's excitement reached the exploding point. "An' if those mortgages were forged, it was just that much written off against the appraised valuation of the land in question. Anything the land brought above the court order was just so much additional velvet. Just a dirty steal!—But how could they get away with it?"

"Assuming that they desired to control a certain parcel of land," Dual resumed, "a copy of an authentic signature might be traced on a spurious document. In many offices to-day there are duplicating devices by which the tracings could be effected. Such a document could then be acknowledged and held in reserve."

"In reserve?" Johnson repeated. "They'd pick up some land they wanted, fake a mortgage on it to one of their gang, and later release it when the title was in their name. Or foreclose on it if they wanted—or maybe forge a deed and have it ready for recordin' as soon as whoever was thought to have signed it was dead. Danged if they wasn't just a bunch of buzzards, waitin' to pick the ribs of dead horses.

"But if they worked it that way, they could loot almost any property they liked. An' if he's been sittin' in that sort of game, no wonder Dobbie was nervous. Forgery ain't exactly child's play, yet. An' the Kenton dame must have known it.—Say! You don't think Dobbie—?"

"CAREFUL, INSPECTOR," Dual admonished. "All this is only assumption. Yet it will, I think, bear investigation. To that end, I shall ask for aid to-morrow morning. Have Quinn examine the records on file at your courthouse. They should show the names of the heirs to these several estates. Through them Dan may gain information to prove our suspicions true or false. There also appears to be a thread leading back to the problem of Miss Kenton's death."

"Ingham!" Johnson said. "Think she knew the papers were crooked?"

"As yet," said Semi-Dual, "we do not know it ourselves. Personally, I do not view Miss Ingham in a criminal light. You can reach her, I understand. Suppose that to-morrow you instruct her to report to Glace. He will bring her to me.—And you, my friend"—his glance swung to Jim—"I will ask to see that Quinn comes to me early for instructions."

I smiled. Here was action—directed action at last. And more, the assurance that in his allocation of a duty to each of us Dual was taking active charge.

"Okay. I'll deliver the frill," Johnson promised.

"And I'll have Dan up here early," Jim added.

"Do so." Dual swept us with his calm gray glance. "The Wheel turns, my friends. Item by item, the balance on the Ledger mounts—and the debtor must meet his debt. Go now, but maintain contact with me until this sorry harvest is gathered, then report at once whatsoever of importance happens."

He paused; his words were a dismissal, but they were more. They were also a promise.

We went out to the garden on the roof. It was dark, and above us swung the star-jeweled Wheel of the Skies. Bryce drew an audible breath.

"Dobbie!" he said. "If he'd broke with Kenton an' she knew too much, and he managed to rub her out—"

"If a lot of stuff you pull was anything but a bowl of cherries—" Johnson growled.

"Pipe down," I said. "The only thing the lot of us are sure of is that Dual knows."

CHAPTER XV

VENUS, DAUGHTER OF LIFE

"**YOUR FRIEND THE** inspector says you wish to see me,"
Gladys Ingham said as she entered my private room, the next
morning.

"Yes," I agreed. "Be seated, please.—Did you work for Jonathan Dobbie, before Miss Kenton employed you?"

"Yes, Mr. Glace," she replied.

"And did you hold a commission as a notary public?"

"And still do."

I saw a question in her eyes.

"And you signed papers for the Realty Investment Corporation?"

"Certainly, Mr. Glace."

"Marge Kenton was in that outfit, wasn't she?" Jim asked.

"Marge!" The girl's tone was startled. "What's happened,
Mr. Bryce?"

"I reckon Dual will tell you," Jim returned.

"As a matter of fact," I interposed, "we asked you here this
morning to take you somewhere else. I want you to see a man
who will probably surprise you. But you will find him very wise."

"A wise man?" She eyed me and smiled. "I've read of them,
but I never saw one."

"You will in a few minutes," I said and rose. "I'm taking you
to him."

A few minutes later, I led her up the bronze and marble stairs to the garden on the roof.

At the top she paused with parted lips and eyes suddenly gone wide.

"What a beautiful penthouse and garden!" she exclaimed. "And what a lovely doorbell! Look at the cute little fountain and the sundial. Oh—this is—marvelous!"

"I told you you'd be surprised. The man who lives here is a truly wise man. I have known him for years, and not once have I had cause to impeach his wisdom. As a chemist deals with reagents, so Semi-Dual deals with the basic life values. Come, Miss Ingham," I said, and led her to that inner room where Semi sat.

Now that room was full of sunlight. Through the great window the light of morning flung a golden aura about the head and shoulders of Dual, in his white and purple robes. Beside me I heard the woman catch her breath as he rose.

"Welcome, Daughter of Life," he intoned. "Thou art Venus—a bright Star in the destiny of him you love. To-day I appeal to you in his behalf.—Be seated. And thou, Gordon, my friend, return when I shall call you."

I understood. On the wall of my private office was a little black telephone box, which was the lower end of a line from Dual's quarters.

I threw Miss Ingham a smile and took myself off.

JUST SHORT of twelve, the phone from the tower buzzed, and I answered and went back to the roof, to find Gladys Ingham changed.

The thing was hard to describe. Yet it was in her face, her voice, her eyes. I had left her a modern woman, independent, self-reliant, a trifle hardened as a result of her contacts with life. And I found her again as one who has gazed, on some unimagined vista that stirred her deeply and would go with her through the years.

I was not surprised. Dual was apt to have some such effect on women, when he wished to win their confidence. Possibly, as he explained it, because women were a trifle closer to the Source, and hence more responsive than men to an expression of the truths of that Universal Force which men call Life.

"You were right, Mr. Glace," she said quietly. "Your friend is a very wise man, indeed."

I nodded. I felt the change the hours had wrought upon her. "You find him different?" I asked.

"Different?" She started to laugh, and caught herself. "I found a terrific intelligence turned on things which I have always thought of as superstitions—and coupled with the understanding of a priest."

"He's given us help in many a baffling case," I said.

"I know." She nodded and sighed. "He told me. I think he's converted me to his creed. He told me things of which I've never dreamed; told me I could help Bob."

That settled it, of course; and I was sure now that Dual, in his subtle fashion, had molded the girl into an instrument of Justice which in his own way he meant to use.

"Just how?" I prompted.

"Oh, dear!" Once more she sighed. "He told me not to say anything, and here I've done it already. It's just that I'm so thrilled to think that I can play even a little part in finding out who really did kill Marge. I can't tell you more than that."

"Then don't," I said. "Dual is a firm believer in the axiom that a closed mouth spills no porridge. However, let me wish you luck."

"Thank you."

She smiled as an elevator came up.

HOW WELL Dual knew life, I thought as I watched her hurry away on the main floor level. So well that he knew how to avail himself of the basic truth that the emotion back of all human action is—self. Some may challenge that statement. But take this girl, as she hastened to what she so plainly felt was the aid of the man she loved. She loved him; wanted him for herself. She might perhaps have resented a suggestion of self-interest. Yet what else was it that made her Dual's ally, in the problem we strove to solve?

I returned to the office, and at lunch Jim and I discussed the things uppermost in our minds. It was after four when Dan showed up.

"Had a day of it," he declared. "Dual sure picks 'em out of the air. I just turned in my report. I wouldn't wonder if Dobbie might have some explainin' to do. He might even need a bonds-man himself."

"Then you got somethin'?" Jim demanded.

Danny grinned. "I got one or two people to askin' questions, at least. Mainly, Dual wanted me to hunt up the heirs of a few estates against which mortgages had been recorded. Naturally, you'd think they'd know something—why a mortgage had been put on, or where the money went to. An' a couple of 'em did. But some claimed they didn't know a thing till the estate was bein' settled; and they're the ones who may build a fire under Dobbie. Most of 'em seem to have figured they couldn't do a thing about it. But a couple of 'em sat up and began to take notice, when I pointed out that the mortgages had been recorded after whoever had signed 'em was dead.

"The maddest of the lot was a bird who says his uncle, the day before he croaked, told him only that he didn't owe a cent. Then when his heir started countin' his marbles, he discovered a plaster worth twenty-five grand on the best bit of real estate he'd inherited. He was stuck, of course. His uncle had died of cancer, and the mortgage had been recorded just ten days before he passed out. But I tell you, he was for makin' war medicine at once! I had to tell him we wasn't sure of anything yet, an' ask him to keep his shirt on till we was. You can bet that any time we want to start sweatin' Dobbie, that baby will cooperate. I gave his address and telephone number, along with one or two more, to Dual.

"He handed me a hot one before I left. Told me to tell you to stick close to Johnson, because unless Mercury delivered his message before one o'clock to-morrow mornin', he was going' to need protection—whatever he meant by that."

"One to-night, huh? At that rate, the show's all set up. Won't be long before something breaks," Bryce said.

"Mercury's the rat." A light of comprehension spread over Danny's face. "Say—I'm goin' down to the Moon to-night an' see what comes off."

"Go ahead," Jim told him. "I don't know where it'll start. But if you see anything suspicious, you might tip us off. We'll probably be at the station, if we're keepin' close to Johnson. Listen, young sleuth. I know how Dual works. Things are comin' to a head. An' no matter where the Jumpin' Jack stands in the killin' of Marge Kenton, that dancin' man is on the spot. That bein' the case, almost anything can happen. So you want to keep awake. Hook up with the tail Johnson's already got on the gig, an' we'll have Johnson put him wise. But if you see anything that strikes you funny, give us a buzz, no matter what Carrigan thinks. Okay?"

"Okay," Quinn assented. The word had a tense sound in his throat.

Then we telephoned the station and got in touch with Johnson.

CHAPTER XVI

GORILLA CONCLAVE

JOHNSON WAS GRUMPY, as we sat together in the detectives' room at the station. Actually he was on edge with the uncertainty of those final hours, wondering what Semi-Dual was up to.

"What's he doing, anyway?" he grumbled. "Why's he stickin' us here on a peg? Why don't he let us grab the gig an' keep him safe? What in hell is the use of takin' chances, if the bird's important?"

"I don't reckon he thinks he's takin' chances," Jim said. "What he said was that Cerra would need protection, unless he delivered his message by one o'clock."

"What message?" Johnson scowled. "I'm damned tired of riddles!"

Jim grinned and lighted a cigar. "You know as much as we do," he said. "We was to report anything that happened."

"Nice!" Johnson growled. "Here we sit and twiddle our thumbs like so many dummies at bridge. If I didn't know him as well as I do—"

"You'd what?" Jim inquired. "Put the gig on ice? Think he'd bust into tears an' sob out his story? Maybe he has got a message to deliver, but that ain't a sign he'd blubber it into your ears. Here's how I figure it out. If what he's expectin' don't happen before one a.m., then the only other play will be to put the Jack where nobody can get at him. Because the Jack's got somethin' that's mighty important, an' he got it out of Marge Kenton's rooms. That's the message Dual is talkin' about. An' if he don't get it by one—"

"Well I'll be damned," Johnson cut him off. "Why ain't you said that before? If Semi can't snag it by the time he's set—"

"Then the gig will be in danger from whoever knows he's got it besides us," Jim resumed. "If Kenton had the goods on Dobbie, for instance, an' the gig had got hold of the evidence, why the thing would be open and shut."

"Only Dobbie wouldn't be fool enough to burn the man down till he had it," Johnson interrupted.

"Sure not, you poor sap!" Bryce assented, grinning. "It's a race between him an' Dual. Only Dobbie don't know it yet. Dual's letting him show his hand."

"Maybe." Johnson appeared to be impressed. "Yep, he might play it that way. It's like him to let a bird hang himself. He gets my goat.—Well, I reckon we follow orders."

WE DID. We sat in that room given over to the strivings of men against crime, and all along we knew that beyond its walls that thing which Dual called the Balance—the sum of action and reaction, of cause and effect—was building its sinister structure. Beyond our observation or knowledge, forces were moving toward a climax.

Johnson was of the police; Bryce and I were at least affiliated with the forces of crime suppression. Yet we sat there passively expectant of results from the machination of one unseen. The effect was odd.

Ten o'clock came, and ten thirty. Now and then the telephone beside Johnson purred; and each time I held myself ready, only to relax again as he spoke on some routine matter.

Then at eleven—a few minutes after—the telephone buzzed again. Johnson grabbed it, jammed the receiver against his ear.

"Johnson speakin'," he growled. "What? Oh—Quinn. Sure, he's here."

*Another
underworld
chief had got his.*

He held the receiver toward Bryce. Jim had it in a single reaching stride, and was speaking.

"Hello, Dan.—You're sure they're Joe's gorillas?—Well, wait a minute." He picked us up with his glance. "Joe's baboons have been filterin' into the Moon, the last half hour, an' Tovallo's bossin' the mob."

"Tovallo, huh?" Johnson's voice was grating. "Here—gimme that thing! This is Johnson. Shoot it."

After that he listened, till at length he spoke again.

"Good boy, Quinn! Go back an' stay on the job. Looks like they was aimin' to throw a scare into Cerra. How's he actin'?—Nervous? Well, maybe he's got a reason. Let us know if anything happens. Okay, son."

His hand slid the receiver back into its cradle. In his eyes there was the look of a hound with his quarry in sight.

"And there you are," he snarled. "Those gorillas are just sittin' there, like a lot of tomcats waitin' for a mouse. That's the way they work, when they're tryin' to break a guy's nerve. The Jack knows they're waitin' for him, an' Dan says he's actin' nervous. Well, he ought to be; he knows he's on a spot. Carrigan's watchin' a car, Dan says. Carrigan says Joe's driver is at the wheel, but it ain't Joe's bus. For two cents I'd send a prowl car to tail it, if the gig's in it when it moves."

"Yeah." Jim spoke with a peculiar rasp. "An' you might send a coupla motorcycles to sweep the street ahead of the procession, too. Accordin' to his brag about the department, Joe oughta rate a police escort at least."

"An' I hope to heaven he gets one to slow music, some day!" Johnson flared.

THE TELEPHONE whirred again, and once more he caught it up.

"Johnson speakin'!—What? Gimme the license number." He scribbled a row of figures. "Okay.—You come in."

Rage and a quickly forming purpose were in his voice.

"That was Carrigan," he rasped. "Tovallo an' a coupla his gorillas just led the Jumpin' Jack outa the Moon, shoved him into that car an' drove off. They beat us to it, damn 'em—but we'll get 'em! I'm puttin' a call through to all prowl cars."

He reached for an inside telephone, but Bryce laid a hand upon the instrument.

"You're puttin' through nothin' till we see what Dual says."

"Oh yeah?" Johnson glared.

But Jim was already calling Semi-Dual's number. We waited,

and then at the sound of an answering voice Jim poured into the mouthpiece the information that Giovanni Cerra had been taken for a ride.

It was all a matter of seconds. I saw Jim's expression alter, saw his interest quicken, saw some of the lines of tension iron out of his face.

"Okay. Sure," he said. "I got it. Let 'em play out their hand, and wait."

He set the telephone aside. An odd grin was on his mouth. It was a thing of gloating satisfaction.

"Never mind that alarm of yours," he said. "Mercury ain't needin' help right now, because he delivered his message before he was grabbed, and that bunch of bums don't dare gun him until they've got it. And they'll get it when Hell is a skating resort.—'Cause why? Dual's got it! Ain't *that* a laugh!"

"Got what?" Johnson demanded.

"The message," said Bryce.

"Yeah. But talk sense, can't you?"

"Nope," Jim grinned again. "I'm tellin' you what he said. I don't know what it is, but it's what Palloni's mob was after. An' all they'll get from the gig is the info that it'll be turned over to the police unless the gig comes back with a whole hide. Semi says to wait, because right now things couldn't be breakin' better."

"Ain't that grand!" Johnson sneered. "If the ride's a washout, all they can do is bring him back. Is that what Dual's expectin'?—If he's got what they want, how in hell did he get it?"

"How do I know?" Bryce grunted for the third time. "The point is, the Jumpin' Jack can't give 'em what Dual's got, and they can't risk bumpin' him off, for fear we'll get it. Of course they don't even know that Semi's alive. Can you beat the way he works?"

"Somethin' he got out of the Kenton frail's flop that night, do you reckon?" Johnson suggested at length, as though speaking his personal thoughts aloud.

"That's my guess," Jim assented, nodding. "An' I bet it will hang the Kenton murderer—"

He broke off as a rap fell on the door. It was opened to admit a police orderly and a girl in a manifest state of excitement. She was Maud Slade, otherwise known as Violet deLisle, the slender, blond leader of the floor show at the Silver Moon.

"Listen, inspector," she began in a panting voice. "I'm in the floor show at the Moon, and Tommy Tovallo and a coupla Joe Palloni's mob jus' took my boy frien' for a ride!"

"**YEAH, I** know all about it," Johnson, cheeked her. "Sit down, Maudie, an' get your breath."

"You know what?"

The woman sank into a chair and stared. Johnson's manner appeared to give her pause. There were smears of make-up still cm: her troubled face.

Johnson answered, smiling, "We know enough to tell you not to get all steamed up about the Jumpin' Jack. Them gorillas will bring him back when they know he ain't got what they want."

"How do you know?"

The girl twisted locked fingers in her lap.

"Nice ring you got, Maudie," Johnson said. "Giovanni give it to you?"

The dancer breathed deeply before she met his glance.

"An' what if he did?" she questioned defiantly. "Say, ain't you goin' to do a thing about Johnnie?"

"We don't need to." Once snore Johnson smiled. "You see, his gettin' rid; of the stuff was just life insurance for Giovanni."

His words were shots in the dark. But they hit the mark. Maud Slade lifted her slender body erect. There was a flare of suspicion in her voice as she exclaimed:

"Say, listen. Is this a frame-up? I thought there was somethin' phony about that girl's comin' to see him this afternoon an' tellin' him about that guy in the penthouse. I suppose that bird's just a pal of yours."

"You talkin' about Miss Ingham?" Bryce questioned sharply.

"Yeah." The dancer threw him a glance. "She was always runnin' around with that Kenton dame."

At last I thought the lines of Dual's endeavor and ours had touched! Gladys Ingham had called on the Jumping Jack and told him about a man in a penthouse!

"So was Johnnie, wasn't he?" Johnson growled.

"Yeah, damn her!" Miss Slade replied. "That is—"

She broke off abruptly.

"He did her dirty work?" said Bryce.

The woman shrugged. "Looks like it wasn't no use stallin'. He never did nothin' much. He just run errands for her."

"Sure. Pickin' up blackmailin' payments," Johnson agreed. "He knocked down five hundred the day she was cooled, didn't he, Maud?"

The woman made no answer.

"Didn't he?" Johnson leaned suddenly toward her. "He bought you that ring you're wearin' with it."

She looked frightened.

"I don't know where he got the price," she lied, glancing at the jewel on her finger.

Johnson struck at her resistance, so characteristic of women of her class. "Listen, kid. We got the low-down on Johnnie. He was in Marge Kenton's flop, the night before she was gunned, and again on the night they knocked her off. What'd he take out of that drawer with the double bottom? Something important enough to make Palloni send his gorillas to take him for a ride."

He paused expectantly.

Still the girl sat twisting the ring around her finger, without response.

"Come on!" Johnson urged. "Kick in, kid. Come clean!"

MAUD SLADE breathed deeply and found her voice.

"Yeah," she said, "it must 'a' been you sent the Ingham twist to pull that same line on Johnnie. I told him she was probably a stool the minute he put me wise."

"And I suppose that's why, when those gorillas edged into the Moon tonight, you got the stuff over to Semi-Dual," Johnson chanced another hazard.

I saw his words strike home, break down the woman's final doubt.

"Semi-Dual, huh?" she said. "Yep. I guess you hold all the cards. There can't be more'n one man with that moniker in the world. It looked like our only out. So—I took it over."

"You took it?" said Bryce.

"Yeah." She eyed him. "Johnnie couldn't, with them heat men watchin' every move. He was hep the minute he seen 'em. An' he says, 'Listen, Sugar—it don't make no difference whether that dame was from the police or not, I'm as good as on the spot right now, if they get their hands on the stuff. But I gotta act like I was dumb. You get it to the fella she told me about.'

"Well, I knew if we couldn't outfox 'em, Johnnie was as good as dead. So I sneak to the dressin' room where I was keepin' it in a trunk, an' I slip out the back way an' grab a taxi an' take it over to this fella on the Urania roof. He's a queer kind of sheik. But he seemed a right guy, at that. He hands me the same line you have about bringin' it to him, bein' the only play to make Johnnie safe. Then he said to beat it back to the Moon, an' if they grabbed Johnnie to come here instead of goin' to our rooms. Said they'd probably search the rooms an' I'd be safer if I did.

"So I lammed it back and went into my dance. And about eleven thirty, Tovallo calls Johnnie to a table where he was sitting with a coupla Joe's men, an' they got up an' Tommy takes Johnnie by the arm, an' they lead him out as quiet as can be, I bet nobody even suspected. But on the level, inspector—do you think he's got a chance?"

"Why, sure," Johnson told her, smiling grimly. "Dual's queer, but he don't make mistakes."

"An' it's a hot sketch any way you look at it," Bryce chuckled. "See here, Miss Slade, what was it Johnnie got out of that girl's flop?"

"Just a book and some papers," the woman said. "I didn't see 'em. But he said there was a lot of stuff in the book about some company, and the papers were mostly mortgages and things like that."

I looked at Jim. A book and papers. It was working out. Strange, how the unescapable Balance built up on Life's Ledger.

"THE REALTY INVESTMENT CORPORATION, wasn't it?" Jim purred.

"I don't know," the woman answered. "But it must 'a' been a graft. Johnnie said that broad told him she had enough on the big shot in it to put him away, if it ever got into court. Said she was lookin' to make a big clean up on it, and that she would put him in on the cut. She was fixin' to marry that sucker O'Neil, an' go to Europe on the jack."

"An' there's your motive," Jim smiled in a twisted way about the cigar in his mouth.

"Plannin' to shake down the big shot, was she?" Johnson addressed Miss Slade.

"Yeah—for half a million."

Johnson glanced at Jim. "An' that's plenty motive," he snarled. "Johnnie knew the market value, and he got the goods the night the girl was gunned. He probably glaumed her gun the night before, when he was in her rooms."

"Johnnie?" The word burst from the woman's lips. "But he didn't! He wouldn't have done such a thing."

"No?" Johnson let her protest hang in the air for a time before he went on. "Five hundred grand will make a man do funny things."

"But—Dobbie?" Jim's tone was a complaining bleat.

"The fall guy," Johnson told him. "Be your age. He pulls Palloni in to help him. He could buy Joe's cooperation for a lot less than half a million."

"But he wouldn't! He didn't!" the dancer denied.

"Says you!" Johnson sneered, "He knew what the stuff was worth—"

The house phone emitted a buzz.

He lifted it to answer. "Yeah? *Cerra?* Bring him in!" His face was a mask of fresh conjecture as he turned to us. "Cerra's outside."

"Johnnie?" Maud Slade gasped.

The door swung open and Cerra stepped into the room.

"Johnnie!" The dancing girl was up and flashing toward him. "Johnnie—what happened?" She caught his arm.

"Wait a minute, kid," he checked, her.

He was a bit disheveled, with tense lids. And his voice was thickened by a conflict of emotions as he spoke to Johnson:

"Look, inspector, Joe Palloni's in my rooms, and he's dead! But I never touched him! I just saw it was him, an' I beat it over here. Because"—he swallowed in convulsive fashion—"they took me for a ride this evening, an' they brought me back. They told me to go up an'—he'd be waitin' for me. He was, only somebody'd gunned him before I got there. It looks like this is the only place I'm safe now."

"John-nie!" Maud Slade sobbed. "Oh—John-nie!"

"Wait!"

In a stride Bryce was at the telephone. Once more he was calling Dual's number, was speaking, listening, voicing assent. Replacing the receiver, he turned his eyes to the dancing man and the girl beside him. He grinned a wolfish grin.

"He says to arrest Cerra," he said quietly.

CHAPTER XVII

HIGH EXPLOSIVE

ODDLY ENOUGH, I experienced no surprise. The unlooked-for part of it was that the man we were told to arrest should have walked into the station as the one place where he might seek safety and be standing before us at the exact moment when the demand for his apprehension was voiced. That was bizarre, yet quite in keeping with the other events of the night, such as the information that Palloni, who had sought to destroy both Cerra and us, was himself now lying dead. The latter fact, however, confused me, because at the time it did not seem to match with anything else.

"Johnnie! Oh, Gawd! Johnnie! You didn't kill him or—that Kenton broad! Tell 'em you didn't!—Johnnie!" I heard Maud Slade half screaming.

"Pipe down, kid—and sit down." Cerra thrust her into her chair. "Well, how about it, inspector?"

He did not seem disturbed.

Johnson nodded slowly before he answered, "Well, if you headed in here for safety, we'd better keep you."

"On what charge?" the dancing man asked.

"Oh, anything from entering Margaret Kenton's rooms the night she was shot to her shooting," Johnson replied. "Right now, I got to go over an' look at Joe. I'd be willin' to give you a medal, if you'd knocked that gorilla off."

He took up the house phone and barked an order for a car, a

photographer, a fingerprint man and a guard. "And send some-body in here," he finished.

The door opened again and an officer appeared.

"Hold these two until I get back," Johnson directed, and rose.

"An' I was wishin' Joe would head a procession, a while ago," he said on the way to the Jumping Jack's rooms. "Danged if I can make head or tail of it, even yet. The Jack never gunned him on a bet. He shows up with just about as much fight in him as a rabbit, an' when we say we're goin' to hold him he seems relieved."

"It might interest you to know that he showed up about two minutes after one," I pointed out.

"The only trouble with that bein' that Dual said he'd need protection *unless* he delivered his message," Johnson growled. "Well, here we are."

We trooped up the stairs, to startle the sleepy attendant in the office on the second floor. Next we were in the rooms to which we had come the night of Margaret Kenton's death. And now they were in wild disorder, with bureau drawers and the door of the single closet open in evidence of a hurried but thorough search. And in the middle of the floor the body of Joe Palloni lay sprawled upon its face. Another underworld chief had got his.

Johnson turned it over. An automatic lay beneath it. The man had been shot through the left breast.

"All right," he said; "get to work."

HALF AN hour later he posted a guard and left. We had found nothing of interest.

"But that ain't surprisin'," Johnson declared. "Nowadays, these birds are hep to everything that used to give us a lead. Anyway, there's one public enemy less."

At the station, the sergeant on duty spoke to Johnson as we came in.

"There was a party called, inspector. Said to ring him when you got back, an' that you would understand."

"Okay. Have Cerra and the Slade girl brought in," Johnson

directed, and went on to the detectives' room. "Go ahead, Jim, and see what Semi wants," he said when the door was closed, upon us.

Bryce complied. He described our fruitless trip to Cerra's rooms, and lapsed into attentive silence finally to utter a promise of compliance and to lay the receiver on its rest.

"He says to book Cerra for murder and to hold the girl as a material witness. Let him know what both of 'em say, the first thing in the morning," he announced.

The Jumping Jack and the dancer were led in.

"Okay. Leave 'em," Johnson said, and sat eying the man and woman till the latter began to fidget and the Jumping Jack wet his lips with his tongue.

"Well, Cerra, the charge is—murder," he said at last.

Cerra nodded. "But I didn't gun him," he denied.

"Nor Marge Kenton?"

"No." The dancing man shrugged.

"Then"—Johnson leaned forward against his desk—"why'd you get the stuff out of that drawer in her bedroom, the night she was gunned?"

"Because she told me to, if anything happened to her," Cerra snarled.

"An' you're expectin' to stand on that?" Johnson asked, at the end of an appreciable pause.

"Sure." Cerra nodded. "She sent for me the night before, and she told me to clean out the drawer if anything happened."

"So you went over and left the cigarette butt on her ash tray?" Johnson growled. "Did you know the stuff was worth a wad of money?"

"Yes." Again Cerra nodded.

"An' you aimed to be in on the cut?"

"Well," Cerra scowled, "she told me I would be, the night before she was shot."

"But she thought the party she was squeezin' might make a play to get her?" Johnson snapped.

"That's the way I doped it," Cerra said, after a pause.

"Who?" The word fairly exploded on Johnson's lips.

"She didn't say."

Cerra looked him straight in the eye; but I saw the fingers of one hand curl, and I wondered if Johnson noticed. If so he gave no sign.

"And you think Palloni was after the stuff?" Johnson said. "Now, tell us about your ride."

Cerra frowned. The change of direction appeared to awaken his suspicions.

Maud Slade broke the silence.

"GO AHEAD, Johnnie. They know the fella in the penthouse; an' anyway, I shot the works."

"Okay, kid."

The Jumping Jack glanced at her blowsy pink-and-whiteness, and turned back to Johnson.

"I'm just a gigolo to you, I guess. But I never rodded Marge Kenton. I just helped her gather the stuff people would pay to have kept quiet. You can pick up a lot of stuff like that in a place like the Moon. An' she had a lot of dirt she'd got when she was a court reporter.—But never mind that. The reason I took the stuff out of that drawer was because I'd told her I would, like I said. I was just a sap about that cigarette.

"But I was nervous when I went there, an' sneaked upstairs an' got into her place with a key she'd handed me the night before. When I dropped a spark on some lingerie in the drawer, I got up an' ditched the fag. An' believe it or not, I never thought of it again till now. I got out of the room, with what I'd come for under my coat, and gave the bundle to Maud. She put it in her trunk at the Moon.

"Then to-day a girl come to see me an' says she's from a guy in a penthouse on the Urania Buildin'. He says my life's in danger, an' my best play is to send him the stuff. I didn't know what to do. I knew the twist. She'd run with Marge a lot, and I knew she was off the deep end about O'Neil. But I wasn't satisfied. She said her party wasn't connected with this office, but was workin' with a coupla private dicks."

"That's me an' Glace, here," said Jim.

Cerra nodded. "Well, I talked it over with Marge," he resumed, "and we doped it out that she'd probably come from you, until to-night. Then, when I seen Joe's monkeys driftin' in, I knew. I was on a spot. I told Maud to sneak the stuff over to the penthouse party the twist had told us about. An' she did. Then Tommy Tovallo called me over to his table, an' him an' two other of Joe's baboons take me out to a car an' drive off.

"But I tell 'em I haven't got the stuff any more, an' if they burn me you'll get it. At first, they don't believe me, but after bit I get 'em worried; an' Tommy stops an' telephones to Joe, I guess, because after that they bring me back to my room an' tell me that Joe is waitin' for me. I go up, an' find him lying there gunned. That scared me, so I get down a fire escape an' lam over here an' bump into Maud. Good thing she come here, too, because I heard Tovallo talkin', an' I know they'd doped it out that she must have the stuff if I didn't, and would slip it to you if they burned me. An' that's all, inspector."

"**WHAT DID** you think, when Tovallo told you Joe was waitin'?" Johnson asked.

"Oh, I figured he'd make me a proposition and then rod me if I was fool enough to accept it," Cerra shrugged.

"The party she took the stuff to told her to come here," Johnson said.

"Yeah?" the dancing man smiled. "Well, I'm glad he's got it. That stuff is dangerous!"

"You're tell in' me!" Johnson grinned, and sobered. "Johnnie, who gunned Palloni?"

"I don't know." The Jumping Jack wet his lips again. "I don't know, inspector. So help me Gawd!"

"Well, all right." Johnson pressed a button. "Take 'em away," he directed when an orderly appeared.

"What do you reckon really happened?" Bryce said when we were alone.

"Write your own ticket," Johnson rasped. "My guess is that Joe was cooled by whoever wanted that stuff. The thing's a wash-out, after the Jack can't deliver an' they don't find it in his flop. And they can't find the girl, because she's with us. So Joe decides to make a deal with Cerra. But maybe he can't do that without authority from the party he's representin'—an'—well, maybe they meet at Johnnie's flop an' have a failin' out. Joe's principal may even have thought he had been double-crossed. Joe was lyin' on top of his gat. They shot it out, an' the other fellow beat it."

"Dobbie, you reckon?" Jim asked.

"I don't know," Johnson scowled. "Maybe Dual will tell us. His hijackin' the evidence by usin' the Ingham doll was a fancy bit of work. That stuff must be high explosive. I've got a hunch this thing is about washed up."

CHAPTER XVIII

HARE AND HOUNDS

YET THERE WAS little to hint of a climax in Dual's garden, the next morning. Before us the cube of the tower showed white in its classic outlines, like some ancient temple of Peace—or perhaps of Justice. A temple housing a priest of that Cosmic Justice that balances men's accounts on the Ledger of Life.

And Dual seemed a priest indeed as we faced him, calm and self-possessed.

"Welcome, my friends, on this last day, 'ere the Debtor shall pay his score."

The last day. My mind caught at his words. The day when the debtor should pay and the sword of Justice fall. And suddenly to my eyes the man before me was like a white-robed Judge, his huge desk a bar of justice.

"The last day, eh?" said Bryce, and his tone was husky.

"Aye," said Semi-Dual. "Tell me briefly of last night, that we may view the events as a part of that pattern which the Shuttle of the Cosmos weaves."

"Palloni's death," he resumed when I had finished recounting what had happened, "is a secondary matter. Yet the hand that slew him also slew the woman, and sent a sum of money with a note protesting O'Neil's innocence."

"You're sure of that?" Johnson challenged.

"Aye," Dual replied. "How should he know of innocence better than by knowing of his own guilt? As a man walks, one step after another, so may one crime lead to another as a consequence. Observe, inspector. A woman dies, and because of that fact her slayer is forced to destroy another, as a measure of safety to himself. Hence Palloni met his fate. It is written that he who lives by the Sword, by the Sword shall that one perish."

"You sure took a slick one in sendin' Ingham to the Jumpin' Jack," said Johnson. "But what if it hadn't worked?"

"If?" Dual repeated. "But, inspector, there was no if. It was an act induced by an impulse given at a time when the one against whom it was directed was ripe because of a problem affecting himself."

"**AND DID** what the Slade girl bring you give you what you needed?" Bryce inquired.

"Practically," Dual assured him. "It remains but to make our final dispositions. And it is possible that as a result of his failure to recover what he required from Cerra, the debtor may make a final and more revealing move, based largely on the fact that Miss Slade is now in jail."

"An' that they don't know a thing about you," Johnson smiled. "D'ye mean he'll try to spring her on a writ an' grab her?"

"The thought occurs," said Semi-Dual. "It is my desire, inspector, that at eight o'clock to-night the principal actors in our drama shall gather here; and that after they are assembled the stairway leading from the upper floor be guarded, to prevent the departure of any one not authorized by yourself."

"Meanin' to shoot, if they need to?" Johnson questioned.

"If the need be," Dual replied. "For to-night, unless I be mistaken, a debtor shall face the score of his debt."

"Okay," Johnson nodded. "I'll arrange it. What else?"

"This," Dual said without hesitation. "I desire that O'Neil, Maud Slade and Giovanni Cerra be present—with Richfield, the gunman Tovallo, and my friends Glace and Bryce."

"Tovallo?" Johnson repeated. "You mean you want him pinched?"

"What need, inspector?" Dual's voice was that of a sentencing judge. "Suppose, rather, that you invite him to be present at a conference in which he will learn the identity of the one who last night slew his overlord. Then should he question your purpose, give him a guarantee that his acceptance does not compass his arrest. Things that are to be will be, inspector, and there must ever be an agent toward the fulfillment of an event."

His words fell in a measured cadence, but I bad no conception of their deeper meaning then.

"Okay," I heard Johnson agree once more. "I'll—tell him."

"There will be others present," Dual said, "but to that I shall attend. And now"—he glanced at the great clock in the corner and drew the telephone from his desk—" learn what has happened at the station during your absence, inspector."

Johnson eyed him oddly as he took the instrument. But he followed orders and gave the number.

"Anything broke since I left?" he asked. And when he had an answer, "He did? Well, hold the line."

He covered the mouthpiece with his palm.

"Richfield's been over to see the Jack an' his girl, an' he left word for me to spring the frill, unless I wanted him to file a writ by noon."

"Admitting his ability to do so, tell him to hold her till you arrive," Dual advised, and waited until the order was given before he resumed:

"**THIS IS** no more than I looked for. With Cerra become fruitless to them, the woman becomes, in their minds, the source of what they seek. Hence, knowing her to be in jail, their logical course is to effect her release. That purpose we may not prevent. But it occurs to me to frustrate its intent. You will therefore release this young woman, hut you will see that she comes to me with the least possible risk of observation. They will be watching for her, inspector. So be forewarned. And in following such a course, we may feel assured that those who desire to remove her from your hands will be confused. For if her whereabouts are secret to them, how shall it fail to disturb them? Do you comprehend?"

"And how!" Johnson grinned. "I'll see that she gets here. An' I'll get the rest of 'em here to-night. What time?"

"As nearly as may be to eight o'clock," Dual returned. "I would suggest that you request Richfield to be present as soon as Miss Slade is released. The press has announced Miss Kenton's burial for this afternoon, and he will probably attend. Hence, he should be informed in order that he may coördinate his plans."

"Okay," Johnson said again. "I'll get on the job."

"But hold on," said Bryce. "Did what that girl brought you show that those real estate deals were crooked?"

"Yes, Mr. Bryce," Dual replied. "But already the morning wanes and a night draws on in which your questions shall all be answered. Go now, and come to me then."

"An' if that don't mean Dobbie's in one tough spot, I don't know what it means!" Bryce declared as we left the roof. "No wonder he wants the Slade twist sprung. Did you notice Dual say there'd be somebody else up here tonight? The old fox! He'll let him fry all day, and then see that he gets a tip he can meet her around eight this evenin', with every reason to feel sure he'll come runnin' to keep the date."

"Our job bein' to get her here," Johnson scowled. "Dual said they'd probably be layin' for her. So why don't you boys get her? I mean, drive down in your car. You can shoot her over easy, an' I'll have a car ready to tail you, just in case anything goes wrong."

"Yeah, we could do it that way," Jim assented.

I GOT my car, while Johnson went to the station, and then we drove down and parked the machine and went inside.

Miss Slade was waiting for us in the detectives' room, and we led her out. That is, we got her as far as the pavement in front of the station. There, suddenly, she whirled and darted back inside.

As by common accord, we followed, to find her standing wide-eyed and panting, her face a terrified mask.

"Say—what's the notion?" Jim began.

She answered, gasping, "That car—it's full of gorillas, wearin' goggles. I saw 'em the minute I went out. They—they're waiting for me. Don't let 'em get me! I—I ain't ready to die!"

"Well, wait a minute," Jim said.

It never occurred to us to doubt her words. There had been a car a dozen yards up the street, as I remembered, and it looked as though we had nearly walked into a trap.

Johnson had heard the girl's excited protests, and he came barging out of the detectives' room, with a question as to what it was all about.

We explained, and Maud Slade panted, "They're Joe's gorillas, I tell you! They was parked and waitin' for me to come out."

"An' it might just be that you're right," Johnson frowned.

He walked to the door and through it, glanced along the street and came back.

"They've pulled off now," he said. "But I reckon they'll be waitin' somewheres close.—I got a way to fool 'em. I got a girl here was brung in last night. I reckon she'll be glad to get sprung for givin' us a little help. She's just about Maudie's size. We'll put her in a car and shoot her out with another one behind her. You drive off, Glace. Those monkeys will see you, and know we're wise. Then, when two cars leave with a woman in one of 'em, they'll figure we're movin' her under guard. We'll drive down the street, an' you watch till you see us pass. Then you drive in behind the station an' pick up Maud. I'll have another car tail yours—not too close, in case they're smart. Okay?"

"Okay," said Jim.

I nodded, went out and got into my car, and drove away. I drove three blocks and parked and waited till I saw a squad car and another car filled with armed men in uniform streak past. Then I drove around the block, slid down to the alley alongside the station and through it to the back. Bryce was waiting for me with Miss Slade, and I saw that they had altered their plans. The little dancer was now clad in hat and coat and pants. She looked like a slender youth as Jim helped her into my machine, together with a bundle which I imagined contained her clothes.

"**STEP ON** it," he said as he swung himself aboard.

We shot out of the alley and off. Jim watched, and suddenly I heard him grunt.

"Smart's right, I guess," he growled in my ear. "I ain't sure, but I think we're bein' followed. Can you get that gray sedan behind us in your glass?"

I nodded. The thing was half a block in the rear, and coming up. I heard our woman companion catch her breath.

The lights went red before me, but I took a chance and shot across the intersection.

The gray sedan followed suit, barely missing the opposite traffic, so that I felt sure that Bryce was right. If so, I knew it would never do to drive directly toward our destination.

I set my foot on the gas, and there followed a game of hare and hounds such as I had never engaged in before. I drove as I had never driven in my life. I dodged and twisted through traffic.

But the gray sedan refused to be lost. One thing and only one sustained me in that race through the city streets, and that was the knowledge of the police car which Johnson had said would be behind us. I shot around a corner on two wheels and straightened out.

"How are we doing?" I questioned.

"Not so good," Bryce answered gruffly. "They darned near went into the curb in gettin' around, but they made it."

"Don't let them get me!—Can't you go faster?" Maud Slade sobbed.

"An' there's the police machine!" Jim exulted, looking back. "They're comin' up fast, an' those gorillas know it. An' they don't want any part of it. They're turnin' off."

In the glass above the windshield, I marked the truth of his words. The gray sedan was just swinging about a corner. I saw it vanish, and eased up on the gas. At the next street I turned in the direction of my original destination, and a minute later a police car ranged alongside.

I saw Mulcahy in it. The machine dropped back.

TEN MINUTES later, I swung up an alley behind the Urania Building and stopped. At its mouth the police car was blocking any other entrance.

I heaved a sigh of relief as Bryce assisted Miss Slade and her bundle to the ground.

"Take her up to our office," I said. "I'll be up as soon as I park."

I left my car where I always kept it, walked back to the building and entered an elevator. I felt oddly tired, and my knees seemed unsteady as I walked. I gained the office and found Jim and Miss Slade in my private room.

"Well, I'm here," she greeted my appearance, "an' I'm darned glad of it! I reckon I gotta thank you an' Mr. Bryce for savin' me from Gawd knows what. If anybody had told me I'd run away from fifty grand, I'd have thought it was a laugh. But what good's fifty thousand iron men, if a bunch of baboons are waitin' to burn you down an' take it back?"

"Meanin' Palloni's mob?" I suggested.

"Who else?" she rejoined. "Johnnie an' me are wise. We might get the jack, but we'd never live to enjoy it. Gosh, was I glad to be in jail this mornin'! An' when I thought they was goin' to turn me out like a cat in a bunch of dogs, was I scared! Till Johnson told me he was sendin' me over to your pal in the penthouse. I had to yes 'em, of course—anyway, I thought so till Johnson showed up."

"Just what happened?" I asked.

"Why, they're dead set on gettin' what I brung over here last night—that book an' the papers," she said. "An' this mornin' that mouthpiece, Richfield, shows up an' says he's authorized to offer us fifty grand. He'll see that I'm sprung so I can get the stuff, he says. Johnnie gives me a wink, an' I say all right; an' Richfield says as soon as I'm sprung to come to his office an' he'll slip me the jack. Then Johnson tells me what's up, an' I get a long breath again—till I see those goggle-wearin' mugs in a car, just as I was goin' out to your machine. When do we go up to your friend's penthouse?"

"Right now," I said, and took her out and rang for an elevator.

I took her up and left her with Semi-Dual. And then I went back to the office to wait for—night.

CHAPTER XIX

THE PLAN

IT CAME THAT last night that was to see the defeat of the one who had fought so desperately, even though under cover, to escape from the penalty of his deeds. Yet save for our anticipations based on Dual's assurance, there was little to hint of the tragic end toward which we moved.

Johnson rang up, late in the afternoon, to say that Richfield had promised to be present and to ask that Jim and I meet him at the station and accompany him and O'Neil and the Jumping Jack to the roof. And that was the way it was done. Jim and I walked to the station, after dining, and found Tovallo with Johnson in the detectives' room. Tovallo was dark and debonair and smiling, with a sangfroid I wondered if he felt. But I saw that under his sleepy looking lids his eyes were as brilliant and watchful as those of a merciless snake.

Richfield arrived, as well dressed as ever, as well poised. He spoke a casual greeting, and seated himself.

Johnson pressed a buzzer and ordered O'Neil and Cerra brought in.

"All set. Come along," he said when they appeared.

"Come where?" Tovallo demanded quickly.

"Where we're goin'," Johnson told him, grinning. "It ain't far, Tommy. Just a matter of a few blocks' ride."

Richfield frowned, but he made no comment as he rose.

We climbed into a couple of cars, Johnson, O'Neil and Cerra, with two patrolmen, in the first; Richfield, Tovallo and Jim and

I in the second. We drove to the Urania and went inside. At the elevator bank, Johnson dismissed the two guards with an "All right, boys!"

Five minutes later, we led our companions into the tower room where Semi-Dual was awaiting our arrival. But not alone. Others were with him: Maud Slade and Gladys Ingham, and three men. Gilroy, Bantum and Farrel, as we were to know them. The first two were well along in years, but were apparently men of substance; the third was young.

Seemingly, Richfield knew them, because he waved Dual's introduction aside as one may with friends. Still, I thought he was surprised at finding them in that tower room, and I thought I marked a swift reaction in the lines of his highly bred face at sight of Maud Slade.

I could scarcely blame him, however. There was the element of surprise in the setting of our meeting—that room with its huge bronze Venus, casting a mellow light on the desk at which Semi-Dual resumed his place when we were seated. And there was certainly something surprising in Dual himself, in his white and purple robes; something judicial in both his bearing and voice as he began speaking:

"**MY FRIENDS** and fellow travelers on the path which men call Life, we are come together to-night to consider a man in the light of his actions; and in so doing to establish a balance against him, to the end that his account on the Ledger of Life shall be closed."

He paused, and his gray glance swept us. My eyes followed the sweep of his. Gladys Ingham was breathing deeply. Maud Slade was staring at Cerra. Tovallo lay back in his chair in a well-nigh indolent fashion, but his alert eyes were on Dual's figure. Richfield sat relaxed with a faint smile on his lips; as though, sybarite that he was, he appreciated the atmosphere and setting of the scene which he was watching.

Dual resumed. "The other night, a woman was shot to death with a weapon which has since been proved to be her own. She was shot in a public resort, while the lights were dimmed for a dance, and her death was not discovered until that dance was done. The time that elapsed was long enough for the one responsible for her slaying to drop the weapon at her feet and go quietly back to his place. This fact, and the additional one that the character of the woman was one to inspire possibly more than one person to aim at her death, and to make suspicion difficult to lodge. For she had been engaging in blackmail and other illegal methods of deriving money from her victims—"

"Stop!" The word burst strangled from O'Neil's throat. He strained forward in his chair as he went on. "I was engaged to Margaret Kenton, and I will not sit here and hear her defamed by any one! I'd be untrue to myself as well as to her if I did not denounce that statement as false!"

"Oh, but it isn't, Bob. It isn't." Gladys Ingham left her chair and took a place beside him. "She did it, Bob. They've proved it. That was how she made her money. I worked for her, and I know. But she loved you, Bob—and I think she meant to go straight for you. I'm—sorry!"

"Gladys!"

O'Neil regarded her out of horrified eyes. He caught her hand and bowed his face upon it.

Dual's glance shifted to Richfield. "Shall we consider the fact that Miss Kenton was engaging in questionable attempts to extort money as established; sir? Or shall! I present further proof?"

Richfield shrugged as he answered. "Let us waive the point, for the present."

Then, to proceed," said Semi-Dual. "Miss Kenton was a most intelligent woman. A court reporter, she graduated from that employment into your office, did she not?"

"Why, yes." Richfield nodded.

"And left your employment later, to establish a business of her own?"

"The Kenton Reporting Service," Richfield assented.

"She was efficient?"

"Very."

"While she was yet in your office, did she act as secretary of the Realty Investment. Corporation?"

"Both while she was there and afterward."

"During the time she was with you, were you acquainted with Joe Palloni, and did you perform legal services for him?"

"Yes, to both questions," Richfield smiled "I'm a lawyer, as you may have been informed."

Exactly." Dual inclined his head "And did you at times assist him in settling out of court matters which might have excited unfavorable reactions if publicly adjusted, but might be suppressed—for a price?"

I HEARD Tommy Tovallo suck in his breath. And Richfield took his time before he answered:

"Whatever my services may have been, they were strictly those of a legal adviser."

"Precisely," Dual agreed. "That is understood. But did Miss Kenton know of these transactions?"

"As my private secretary, she may have." Once more Richfield shrugged. "But I understood we were to consider her—er— death; rather than her former life."

"Yet," said Semi-Dual, "it falls out that we may at times follow example to our detriment or the reverse. The false hare of easily gotten fortune has proved the downfall of many a life."

"Say—!" Tovallo suddenly snarled, "Is dis a church?"

I sensed tensing muscles, and all at once to me the man was like a dangerous, crouching beast.

Dual, however, seemed undisturbed. He continued, "What we seek to establish is that even when she was in Attorney Rich-field's office, Margaret Kenton knew Joe Palloni. She came to see, by example, how readily illicit profits might be made; and at the same time she became secretary of the Realty Investment Corporation, an organization the operations of which were open, to question at least. We have sworn evidence in support of both assertions."

"SWORN?" RICHFIELD shifted himself and sat erect.

"Aye. It can be produced, at need."

"And exactly what do you mean by saying that their operations were open to question?"

"That they were designed to, derive a profit through the purchase and sale of properties against which claims in the form of forged mortgages had been, recorded—Mr. Farrel," Dual addressed the younger of the three men we found on our arrival, "have you, or have you not, reason to agree with me that in the settlement of your uncle's estate you may have been victimized?"

"About twenty-five thousand dollars' worth of reason," the man declared, without hesitation. "Richfield settled the estate. And despite the fact that Uncle Dick told me that everything was clear, the first thing we ran up against was a mortgage for twenty-five thousand, executed and recorded just a few days before his death. You haven't forgotten that, have you, Richfield?"

"Certainly not," the lawyer responded, frowning. "But I recall nothing to indicate that the document was what our—er—host calls spurious, or, as I assume he may mean, forged."

"Perhaps not in the specific instance," Dual said before Farrel could speak. "You are legal adviser to Mr. Gilroy, and to Mr. Bantum also, are you not?"

"In so far as I know." Richfield glanced at the two men and smiled.

"And as such you are more or less familiar with their affairs?"

"More or less, I think, would cover the situation."

"Then were I to tell you that among Miss Kenton's papers mortgages had been found against certain of their holdings, apparently signed by themselves, but of which they deny all knowledge, what would be your opinion as to the authenticity of those documents, neither of which have as yet been recorded?" Dual inquired.

"I'm afraid I would need to discuss the matter with my clients before risking an opinion." Richfield evaded a direct answer, and then he turned to Gilroy and Bantum. "Gentlemen, do you know that such documents exist?"

"There isn't a doubt of it, Richfield," Gilroy told him. "Both Bantum and I have seen 'em."

"Then," Richfield set his lips, "all that I can say is that I'm— amazed."

"ENOUGH OF it, then, for the present," Dual thrust the matter aside. "In the beginning I spoke of the Ledger of Life. The allusion was something more than a symbolic mouthing of words. We of the material world to-day are walking blindly. In the Spectrum of Universal Force, there are forces which maintain not only the equilibrium of material things, but a spiritual balance also, and measure to each man according to his deeds. In the specific instance, we have an example of the operation of this law, from which no man may escape. Margaret Kenton brought her death upon herself. Yet he who slew her incurred a debt in her slaying. A debt is a debt, and must be paid. Observe how the items mount on the Ledger.

"Miss Kenton was a woman of ability, in no appreciable measure swayed by the emotion which men call love. As a court reporter, she attracted the attention of a man of brilliant mind, Attorney Richfield, who took her into his office. The picture begins to change. Much of Attorney Richfield's practice, as he must admit, is drawn from the so-called underworld. In his office she met Joe Palloni; she saw how readily human mistakes might be turned to selfish advantage. She fell under the spell of craftily gotten wealth, and when the Realty Investment Corporation was organized she knowingly engaged in its criminal operations. Later, she engaged in blackmail, using information gained as a court reporter, and in other ways, to enrich herself. Giovanni Cerra assisted her both in the collection of such information and in the collection of the monies which her victims paid. Is this really true, Cerra?"

"Yes." The word was a whisper.

"And now," said Semi-Dual, "we find Margaret Kenton faced by a thing which she had heretofore laughed at. She fell in love with Robert O'Niel. Life changed for her. She dreamed of gaining a sufficient sum and forsaking her former ways; of marrying the man of her choice and leaving the country. Of this she told him only part She alleged that she was about to inherit a fortune; in reality, she planned to capitalize her knowledge of the realty company's illegal transactions.

"She knew the criminal facts; knew that they were damning enough to rum the man they most nearly involved; knew herself to be in a position to prove them; further, that although she had profited through their joint endeavors, his profits had been vastly larger, since at the time the corporation was formed the stock of the several incorporators who were figureheads really, was immediately assigned by them to the individual by whom the plan and its purpose was conceived. Consequently, she knew him to be rich, and she saw in his fear of exposure and possible loss of freedom the means to the respectable life which she now desired. Of him she demanded a fortune, as the price of silence.—Do I hold your interest?"

"Yeah, plenty! I begin to smell a mouse," Tommy Tovallo answered.

CHAPTER XX

CLOSED ACCOUNTS

HIS EYES MET those of the man at the desk, and held them. To me, it was as though Dual was reading the gangster's thoughts—those intangible, short, electro-magnetic waves which the working brain gives off.

"And if I were to tell you your suspicions were correct?" he said at length.

The gunman scowled.

"I don't know but what I'd believe you. An' I'd sure get a laugh at bein' so dumb that I didn't think of it last night," Tovallo snarled.

"Last night," said Semi-Dual, "you returned from a mission that failed, to find Joe Palloni dead."

"Yeah." Tovallo nodded. "You're a plenty wise guy, I guess. When Johnson told me you'd put the finger on the rat what cooled him, I wasn't so sure you wasn't bluffin'. But just the same, I wasn't passin' the chance that you might be shootin' straight. And now—"

"Now," Dual interrupted, "you're beginning to see that I never make a statement I am unable to support. Hence, in your own words, Signor Tovallo, let us get on with it. Margaret Kenton demanded five hundred thousand dollars—practically half of their ill-gotten profits—from her former associate, and—"

"Five hundred thousand!" O'Neil cried thickly.

I knew that he was thinking of what the woman he loved had

told him of a supposititious inheritance. The amounts were the same, as he must appreciate.

Dual ignored his evident emotion.

"Margaret Kenton died," he continued, "and Mr. O'Neil was arrested for her murder. Attorney Richfield, who was present in the Silver Moon at the time, though he expressed the opinion that Miss Kenton's death might have been an act of self-destruction, volunteered as her friend and former employer to act in Mr. O'Neil's defense. The next day, he learned of a will naming Mr. O'Neil as Miss Kenton's heir; and my friends, Glace and Bryce, were asked to attempt an investigation in Mr. O'Neil's behalf.

"They conferred with Mr. Richfield, and arranged to make a search of Miss Kenton's apartment that night. But on their way to the Willden Apartments, an attempt was made to force a car containing themselves and Inspector Johnson off the West Park viaduct, so that their arrival was delayed. Attorney Richfield was waiting for them in Miss Kenton's rooms, when they finally arrived. The search was made, and a book containing memoranda applying to certain cases at law was discovered. It was in an investigation of these members that suspicions concerning the transactions of the Realty Investment Corporation were aroused.

"Furthermore, on the second day after the murder, Glace and Bryce received five hundred dollars in one-hundred-dollar bills together with an anonymous letter instructing that they be used in proving O'Neil's innocence. This is important because of the fact that a certain woman who loves him chanced to see, in a town to which she drove with a companion on the evening before, a man who might possibly have mailed the money. Later, Attorney Richfield expressed the opinion that the money might prove of value in gaining Mr. O'Neil's acquittal.

"Hence, it appears that the letter containing the money may have been actually sent by the person who slew Margaret Kenton, in an endeavor to throw suspicion upon Giovanni Cerra. However, that was at a time when the sender was unaware that in purchasing a ring for Miss Slade, with currency traced through its serial numbers, Cerra had unwittingly discounted the expected effect in advance.—Miss Ingham, you will swear that on the night in question you saw this man in the town where the letter was mailed, will you not?"

I MARVELED at Dual's complete weighing of every phase of the problem with which he was dealing. Gladys Ingham answered, "Yes, sir," without lifting her downcast eyes.

"And now," Dual's voice took on a strange, metallic and measured quality not unlike the click of some mechanical device, "behold how the Score of the Debtor grows on the Cosmic Ledger. From now on, I shall make no statement not substantiated by our investigations, or by evidence within our possession, or capable of substantiation by the word of actors involved in the matter. On the day before Miss Kenton was slain, two letters, later proved to have been written upon a machine in the dead woman's office, were brought to Glace and Bryce. One of these earlier letters demanded five hundred dollars for the suppression of certain facts in a man's private life. Did you receive that sum from a young man on the corner of Spring and Mason Streets at noon on the day before she was murdered, Giovanni Cerra?"

"Yes," Cerra replied.

"And did you give the money to Miss Kenton?"

"No." The Jumping Jack wet his lips. "She was dead before I got a chance."

"So you used a part of the sum to purchase a ring for Miss Slade, as I have already stated?"

"Yes," Cerra nodded.

"The other letter," said Semi-Dual, "was to a young woman, who showed it to Joe Palloni. Palloni appeared to know the writer, because he declared that if she tried to interfere with his activities, he would, as he expressed it, 'put the heat on her' himself. Hence, when this young woman—who is a self-admitted heiress—was abducted, suspicion turned upon Palloni, and he consulted you, Mr. Richfield, did he not?"

"Quite right," Richfield said.

"I mention the matter chiefly because it was through these letters that Margaret Kenton's blackmailing activities were first suspected," Dual went on. "Do you see how each item takes its place? On the night before her murder, Miss Kenton had told Giovanni Cerra to remove certain evidence from a hiding place in her bedroom, in case anything happened to her. She gave him a key to her rooms, if the need arose. Surely such action, added to the further fact that she made a will in Robert O'Neil's favor, may be taken as an indication that she felt herself in danger, may it not?—Giovanni Cerra, when you were in her rooms the night before the murder, did she name the man she feared?"

"She didn't say—who it was," Cerra stammered. "But she said she was leavin' somethin' along with the other stuff to show who done it—if anybody—did."

SOMETHING LIKE a sigh ran through the room. The atmosphere, all at once, was electric, as we waited for the total of that account on the Ledger of Life to mount, and knew it to be nearly complete.

"And did she?" Dual asked.

"Well—yes." The words seemed actually to be forced from Cerra's throat. "Anyway, she left a statement she'd made out and sworn to before Miss Ingham."

"As a notary?" Semi questioned. "Is that true, Miss Ingham?"

"I—I suppose so," Gladys Ingham replied. "But—I didn't know what it was when I took her acknowledgment. It was a rather lengthy paper, and I didn't read it."

"But you had signed other papers for her, some of them for the Realty Investment Corporation?" Dual prompted.

"Yes, sir."

Silence followed the words. Once more Dual's eyes were turning on us. Tiny flecks of light were in them. Demand was in his voice as he added:

"Do you see how the Balance builds and builds? Did you read that document, Giovanni Cerra?"

"Yes, sir, I did," Cerra answered hoarsely.

Richfield interrupted with "One moment, please! If you know the identity of the woman's slayer, why is he still at large?"

"Have I said that I knew it?" Dual questioned. "Or can we count the affidavit of a woman dead as proof of an action which in life she feared? Yet it may point a finger of suspicion, and the document in question was delivered to me last night."

Once more, I heard the hiss of Tovallo's breathing. Dual swung to him.

"It was delivered to me, Signor Tovallo, before you took Giovanni Cerra from the Silver Moon, in a car for which Joe Palloni's chauffeur was the driver. That was before Joe Palloni had died, too. It's importance is twofold—first as showing that the moral decay of the woman who wrote it is largely due to the influence and example of the man on whom her demands were made; secondly, as showing the means by which her own weapon came into his possession. That part of it I shall read."

HE PRODUCED a folded paper from a drawer of the desk and spread it before him.

"She says: 'I told him I would publish the truth of the Realty Investment Corporation steals unless he agreed to my terms. He told me he'd see me dead first, and started to his feet with an expression which made me think that he intended a personal violence. I ran into my bedroom for a weapon, but he followed, twisted my automatic from my grasp and laughed: "You little fool, do you think I'd do it here?"'— Did you read this, Giovanni Cerra?"

"Yes." Once more Cerra voiced a throaty assent.

"Then why did you not take it to the police?"

"I—well, I figured it was worth a lot, an' that if I could hold it till some of the smoke blew away I might be able to cash in on it myself," the Jumping Jack confessed.

"Exactly." Dual laid the paper aside. "And now to return to the night of Margaret Kenton's death. The man she named in this paper was in the Silver Moon, both before and after she died. It is known that Miss Kenton sent her escort to the check room, ostensibly for a bag which she said she had placed in his overcoat pocket—despite the fact that the bag in question was in her possession at the time.

"Why did she do such a thing? We may only assume. Yet we know by her slayer's own admission that she had seen him; that a sign of recognition, a signal perhaps, had passed between them; and we assume that she felt little fear of him in so public a resort. Hence she sent Mr. O'Neil away so that she might speak with her former associate without Mr. O'Neil's knowledge. During Mr. O'Neil's absence, her slayer went to her table; and having shot her, he returned to his seat and waited until her death was discovered, so that he might become no more than one of the horrified group of men and women who gathered about her. But herein was he tricked. Though the woman was dead, he must yet obtain possession of the evidence which she had possessed, and which even yet could blast him as completely as though she were alive.

"Toward its possession he took steps. But we, on the other hand, foresaw them and took others. Giovanni Cerra received a message that its possession endangered his life; and last night, when he knew that Signor Tovallo and other members of Joe Palloni's organization were moving against him, he sent it to me by Miss Slade.—Giovanni Cerra, what happened after the Signor Tovallo and his companions were convinced that it was no longer in your possession last night?"

"Tommy telephoned to some one," Cerra said.

"Did you telephone Palloni, signor?" Semi asked.

"Sure," Tovallo assented. "I told Joe dis rat said if we burned him dicks would get de stuff. An' he says bring back de rat; dat he'd get in touch wid de big shot an' tell him he'd hafta make a deal wid de rat an' gun him afterwards. He said he expected de boss would be all steamed up, but he'd get hold of him an' they'd handle de rat at his flop. So—we took him back. When Joe said to do a t'ing, we done it."

"And—Palloni and this man were waiting?"

"Waitin'? Hell! You know how he was waitin', all right," Tovallo snarled.

AGAIN THERE came a momentary pause. Then Dual laid both hands on the desk before him and leaning a trifle forward, resumed:

"What happened in Giovanni. Cerrra's room is a thing at which we can only guess. However, we may assume that the slayer of Margaret Kenton was by then no longer his normally balanced self; he was disturbed, by his failure to obtain the thing upon which his position, his reputation, his very, freedom depended. There may have been a falling out—he may have felt that he had been, or was being, betrayed by a man he had served as a criminal for years. Palloni died with his own weapon beneath him. And with this I think our case against the Debtor is well nigh complete.

"Your opinion, Attorney Richfield? Am I justified in accusing you not only of the murder of Margaret Kenton, a girl whose moral integrity you had debased, a girl who left your employ because she would not consent to your stealing her body as well as her soul, but in addition the shooting of Joe Palloni?"

Richfield took it without a quiver of his well bred face. Ever the poised, self-possessed lawyer, he was cool and collected. There was even a smile of something like taunting admiration on his lips as he replied:

"I'm afraid not, Mr. Dual. As you have so ably pointed out the affidavit of one—er—deceased concerning a threat alleged to have been uttered, or of fears aroused by such a threat, is not proof that the threat was actually carried out. No, strong as you make it appear, in your masterly but somewhat wearisome presentation, and speaking as I do without time for a fuller consideration, your case in a modern court would, in my presentation, scarcely prove strong enough."

The speech was both defiant and challenging; and Richfield meant it as such, of course. The man amazed me. Faced by Dual's accusation, made almost casually as a question, he met it, voiced the opinion it pointedly called for, and left his accuser to speak. Against every inclination, I was forced to admire his unshaken nerve. And then, in the moment of straining tension that followed it was Tommy Tovallo's voice that lashed at him like a whip.

"Naw, you rat! Maybe not in a court. Dey're a laugh an' both of us knows it. But our mob fries its own fish!"

He fired from the hip, without rising, without even drawing his hand from the pocket of his coat. I had seen it there, but had not suspected what it held: But now, as the muffled report of the weapon stabbed through the room and Richfield's body twitched to the impact of the bullet and sagged in its chair, he drew the gun out and sprang to his feet.

Gladys Ingham screamed.

"Sit still, youse!" Tovallo's voice rasped above her outcry. "He asked for it, an' he got it. But I don't want to burn nobody else, and I won't if you act wise.—T'anks, Mr. Dual. You're a right guy, an' you keep your word. Dat's right, folks, take it quiet. I'm washed up here, an' I'm leavin'."

He backed through the door.

JOHNSON LEAPED from his chair and drew a service automatic.

Dual's hand pressed a button on his desk. "Quiet!" he admonished. "The garden is lighted. He cannot escape."

Crash! Crash! The sound of shots drifted out of the night from the stairhead, where Johnson's guards were posted, then silence followed. Through how many lagging seconds it lasted I do not know. And then Semi-Dual rose in his white and purple robes, like a judge returning to his chambers.

"It is ended," he intoned. "From the Court of Cosmic Justice there is no appeal."

Johnson nodded and left the room; Bryce and I followed. The garden was flooded with light. Near the stairhead, two burly figures were bending above a third, sprawled upon the path. We went toward them, and they straightened at our approach.

"He run right into it, sir," one of them spoke to Johnson. "We heard a shot, an' the lights come on. He run out with a gat in his hand, and you'd told us to shoot, if we had to. He's stone dead."

"It was comin' to him," Johnson said. "He'd just shot Attorney Richfield."

"Yeah?" the patrolman commented gruffly. "Well then, I guess this will balance the account."

His words arrested my attention, seemed grimly appropriate.

"Yes," I agreed, "the account is balanced."

Bryce gave me a glance, but he spoke no word.

"Stay here," Johnson directed. "I'll telephone the station."

We went back inside the tower. Richfield's body still sat in his chair, but some one had dropped a handkerchief over his face. Maud Slade and Cerra were huddled together, and the girl was sobbing in a dry, reasonless choking way. Gilroy and Bantum and Farrel were conversing in lowered tones to one side.

Johnson approached Dual. "May I use the telephone?" he asked.

Semi-Dual drew the instrument from his desk.

"Richfield was Mars?" I said.

"Aye," Dual assented.

Gladys Ingham sat beside Bob O'Neil. Her arm was about him. She had drawn his head to her breast. And for all his six feet of manhood, he was letting it lie there, unashamedly, like the head of a child that is tired.

"I—didn't know, Gladys. I didn't know!" I heard him repeating.

Dual approached them as they sat there. He stood beside

them and placed his hand on the woman's shoulder. She lifted her face.

"Daughter of Life, you have served. The Balance is in your favor. It brings you your reward," he said.

ABOUT THE AUTHOR: DR. J.U. GIESY

BORN NEAR CHILLICOTHE, Ohio, August 6, 1877. That makes me a Buckeye, and some people have suggested that I was a nut. Of my actual birth I have no recollection. So this is mere hearsay evidence. When I was eight months of age my parents removed to southeastern Kansas and took me with them, as I was still unable to shift for myself.

When I was thirteen we again removed to Utah, where I received my common school education in common with other youngsters of a similar age. In 1895, I entered the Starling Medical College, Columbus, Ohio, and received my medical degree from that institution in 1898.

Returning to Salt Lake, I served an interneship in a local hospital and have practiced medicine in that city ever since, with the exception of the time I spent in the United States service during the World War as a captain in the Medical Corps. As regards the Army I am still a major in the Reserve, attached to the Division Surgeon's Office of the 104th Division. In 1916 I was instrumental in organizing the first Plattsburg camp ever held in the State, starting the movement and acting as secretary of the general committee which put it over.

I began to write in 1910. Unlike many well known writers, I have had rejections since. At the same time I've found a lot of editors who liked my work. I have written as an avocation ever since. At present I am associate editor for Utah on the staff of *California and Western Medicine*, and the staff of the

Archives of Physical Therapy X-Ray and Radium. Because of the latter fact I am a member of the American Medical Editors Association.

I am also a member of the Salt Lake Chamber of Commerce, and a life member of the American College of Physical Therapy, which I have served as an officer for several years. My ancestors made me a Son of the American Revolution, and I have made myself more or less of a nuisance to a lot of people all by myself.

J.U. Giesy

I was married in San Francisco, to Juliet Galena Conwell, in December, 1904, and the marriage took. Personally I think they did better work along those lines, that long ago. Anyway we're still living in the same apartment, with no intentions of divorce.

Just why the editor should want to print this confession I really can't imagine. But that's his business. He's asked for it and here it is!

ABOUT THE AUTHOR: JUNIUS B. SMITH

I WAS BORN at Salt Lake City, Utah, September 29, 1883, at approximately 3:55:27 P.M., right ascension of the mid-heaven (for the benefit of my astrological readers) 16 hrs. 27 min. 57 sec., or 246° 59' 15"; position of planets, Neptune 20° 45' ret. Taurus, Saturn 10° 6' ret. Gemini, Mars 22° 10' Cancer, Jupiter 0° 26' Leo, Moon 22° 24' Virgo, Uranus 24° 34' Virgo, Sun 6° 27' 23" Libra, Venus 8° 52' Libra, Mercury 20° 31' ret. Libra. Declinations: Sun 2° 34' south, Moon 0° 7' south, Neptune 16° 13' north, Uranus 2° 50' north, Saturn 20° 2' north, Jupiter 20° 18' north, Mars 22° 25' north, Venus 2° 20' south, Mercury 11° 17' south.

With this meager astronomical data, the astrologians will know more about me than I could write in a volume.

For the benefit of you other readers:

I am an attorney at law and practiced for many years, paying my office expenses in the lean years by writing. I never had the bitter experience of having to write years before anything sold. At the beginning of my writing career, Dr. J.U. Giesy and I joined intellectual forces, and our first joint effort was submitted to *Argosy* way back in 1911. It sold, first time out. Rapidly we "dashed" off more and they sold also. We each write separately as well as jointly, at such times as we cannot get together.

Early in life I took up astrology as a hobby and lived to see it recognized in judicial decisions as a science. That I have helped, in some measure, to brush away the misconceptions in the minds of many people regarding this much maligned subject

is perhaps testified to by my elec-
tion to Fellowship in the American
Academy of Astrologians, an organization that one can't get into for
the asking.

I've wasted enough time playing
checkers to have built one of the
Egyptian pyramids single-handed.
Another hobby is shorthand, which
has fascinated me for thirty years.
I understand several systems. I can
sling a wicked toe on the dance
floor, but only dance when my
weight crowds two hundred. One
year I spent the summer on the
desert drying out, where my own

Junius B. Smith

cooking, plus the heat, effected a material reduction. But I come
honestly by it: my father weighed two hundred and sixty in
athletic condition—three hundred when not.

And speaking of ancestors: My grandfather was a brother of
Joseph Smith, who founded the Mormon Church, which probably explains why I was born in Utah.